Hamilton Wright Mabie

My Study Fire

Hamilton Wright Mabie

My Study Fire

ISBN/EAN: 9783337250867

Printed in Europe, USA, Canada, Australia, Japan

Cover: Foto ©Andreas Hilbeck / pixelio.de

More available books at **www.hansebooks.com**

MY STUDY FIRE ** BY HAMILTON WRIGHT MABIE
SECOND SERIES...

NEW YORK: PUBLISHED BY
DODD, MEAD AND COMPANY
MDCCCXCV

𝔘niversity 𝔓ress:

JOHN WILSON AND SON, CAMBRIDGE, U.S.A.

TO

LORRAINE

AND

HELEN

CONTENTS.

———•———

MY STUDY FIRE.

THE BOOK AND THE READER.

MRS. BATTLE, intent upon whist, insisted upon "a clear fire, a clean hearth, and the rigour of the game." The veteran reader, who has come to love his occupation not only for what it gives him but for itself, is equally punctilious; he must have a quiet room, a cheerful blaze, and the book that fits his mood. He has meditated before the fire, book in hand, so many silent and happy days that he knows all the subtle adjustments which a man may make between himself and his library. I rarely look at my books in that leisurely half-hour which precedes getting to work without fancying myself at the keyboard of an organ, the pipes of which are the gilded and many-coloured rows on the shelves about me. One may have any kind of music he chooses; it is only a question of mood. There is no deep harmony, no haunting melody, ever heard by the spirit of man which one may not hear if he knows his books thoroughly. The great · gales that swept Ulysses into unknown seas, and the soft winds that stirred the myrtles and brought down the pine cones about Theocritus are still astir, if one knows how to listen. And those inner melodies which the heart of man has been singing to itself these thousands of years are audible above all the tumult of the world if one has a place of silence, an hour of solitude, and a heart that has kept the freshness of its youth.

The quality which makes a reader master of the secret of books is primarily of the soul, and only secondarily of the mind; and to get the deepest and sweetest out of literature one must read with the heart. A book read with the mind only is skimmed; true reading involves the imagination and the feelings. And it is for this reason that one needs to select a book for the day, instead of taking the first one that comes to hand. If one reads simply as a mental exercise or for information, one book is as good as another; but if one reads for personal enlargement and enrichment, every hour has its own book. There are days for Sir Thomas Browne and days for Lamb — although I am often of opinion that all days are for Lamb; there are days for Shakespeare and days for Wordsworth, days for Scott and days for Thackeray. The great days when one is buoyant, fertile, virile, belong to the great writers. Emerson says, with regard to that difficult dialogue of Plato's, the "Timæus," that one must wait long for the fit hour in which to read it: "At last the elect morning arrives, the early dawn — a few lights conspicuous in the heavens, as of a world just created and still becoming — and in its wide leisure one dare open that book." These hours of health and vitality belong to Dante, Shakespeare, and Goethe, and their kindred. The morning hours are due to the mountain summits, and it is a sad waste to bestow them on any outlook narrower than the horizons. But there are other days, hardly less profitable, when one does not stir with the lark, but lingers under the shadow of the roof-tree ; and for these more subdued hours there are voices equally musical, if not so compelling, voices of personal if not of universal truth. A reader of catholic temper will welcome all the great spirits at his hearthstone, and will leave the latch-string out for the new-comer whose name still lingers in that delightful obscurity which precedes fame.

It is a mistake to read too many books, to permit the habit of reading to obscure the ends of reading ; but it is equally a mistake to read exclusively in a very few directions. There are people whose egotism transforms their very faults into virtues, and who imagine that their love of books is profound because it is limited. One can have but few intimate friends, but it is wise to choose these friends from among the greatest, and especially from among those whose temperament, habit, and surroundings are different from our own. It was said of Dr. Mulford that he was narrow on great lines ; the difficulty with many men is that they are narrow on small lines. It is wise to follow one's taste, for that is the line of least resistance, but it must not be forgotten that what is commonly called taste is not necessarily good taste ; it is merely personal inclination : good taste involves education. Our companions

of the mind ought, therefore, to be, not those who
confirm us in our preconceptions and build our limitations still more massively about us, but those who lib-
erate us from the defects of our nature and the faults
of our training. "Our friends," says Emerson, "are
those who make us do what we can." The friend who
entertains us is welcome, but if he does not pass
beyond that stage in our intercourse he never really
touches what is deep and individual in us; there is no
real commerce of soul between us. The wise reader,
therefore, will not always turn to one corner of his
library, but will pass from shelf to shelf, and will know
best those who are best worth knowing.

Those only who can command the highest pleasures
of life — solitude, leisure, and books — are able to
realize the temptations which beset the reader and lure
him often from the strait and narrow way which leads
to the deepest and richest intellectual life. Sitting in
slippered ease before a merry fire, the earth white to
the horizon, the air keen as that at Elsinore, bells in
the distance and silence and warmth within doors, one
feels the danger of becoming a callous monopolist.
The consciousness that one is steeping his mind in
pure comfort, in unmixed delight, while most men are
toiling in offices and rushing about crowded streets,
sometimes breeds a dangerous sense of being favoured
of fortune. The scholar has ever been the most fortunate of men, because he is free to pursue the things of
the mind, while his fellows are compelled to pursue
the things of the body. But the scholar is sometimes

as arid as some men of affairs, as juiceless and unin-
teresting as some capitalists. Acquisition for its own
sake develops the same quality of character whether
one devotes himself to the hoarding of money or of
facts. There is, however, a largeness, a vitality, about
books which helps one against the very temptations
which they present to the man who loves them. To
read for the mere luxury of reading is to miss the best
things which they have to give. In every true companionship there is an interchange; one gives as well
as receives. The best reading — the most intelligent
and fruitful — involves a community of interest and
thought between the reader and the writer; the con-
tribution of the latter is positive, and that of the former
negative, but both are real and both are necessary.
The actor speaks in vain unless the imagination of the
theatre kindles and co-operates with him. In every
audience there are listeners who have almost as much
to do with the speaker's felicity and eloquence as he
has himself; they are persons who listen actively, not
passively. There are readers who hang like dead
weights on the skirts of a writer, and there are those
who walk beside him buoyant with his strength, eager
with his energy of spirit, and kindled with the glow of
his thought. These are the readers who make a true
exchange with the writer, who are not weakened by
many books, who select the best, and become companions of the heart as well as of the mind.

THE READER'S SECRET.

ONE of the secrets of the artist is the facility and completeness with which he turns his conscious processes of mind into unconscious ones, and so does without effort that which costs a man less thoroughly trained no little toil. To do with ease what one began to do with effort is to have passed from the state of the artisan to that of the artist. Art involves the hardest kind of work, but in its essence it is play; for it is always an overflow of the creative force of a rich nature, and never power strained to the last point of endurance. A great picture, poem, or symphony always leaves the impression of something behind richer and profounder than that which it conveys; it makes one conscious, as Ruskin has said, of a great power rather than of great effort. A man is never master of his material and his art until they have become so much a part of him that he can hardly separate himself from them. The material has been absorbed by his imagination and brooded over so long that it becomes his own by the only absolute right of possession known among men. So Shakespeare took the story of the "Tempest" as he found it in some Italian or Spanish tale, and meditated upon it until the whole wealth of his nature passed into it and the bare framework became incrusted with such pearls as lie only in the great deeps of such a heart as his. The art has been so lovingly studied and so loyally practised that it becomes a skill of the soul rather than a dexterity of the hand, and what was at first calculated with nicest sense of proportion and adjustment becomes at last a natural and almost effortless putting forth of strength.

Now, the trained reader who has mastered his art passes through a kindred progress from the conscious to the unconscious. He begins with rules, times, and habits; these are the mechanical side of his training; but when he has learned his craft he has long ago forgotten them. The artist's education is of supreme importance to him; but when he comes at last to handle his brush with creative freedom and force, the processes of his training are as far behind him and out of his thought as is the hard discipline of learning one's letters out of mind when one is deep in " Henry Esmond " or " The Tale of Two Cities." The conscious process has become unconscious; that which one began to do as work he now does as play. The attitude of the reader toward his book is at last one of unconscious receptivity; his intelligence is keenly awake and active, but it has ceased to be conscious of itself; the whole nature is absorbed in the book. This means true reading, — reading, not for entertainment, but for personal enrichment and enlargement. One may skim a book as a swallow skims through the air and leaves no trace of its flight; or one may build a nest in a book and make it one of the homes of the spirit in the brief summer of life. The great works of the imagination ought to be part of our lives as they were once of the very substance of the men who made them.

To see only the splendid pageantry of the Shakespearean drama is to suffer the eye to cheat the imagination. Shakespeare speaks to that which is deepest and most individual in us ; his word is for the soul, not for the ear only. To catch the matchless music of his verse is, indeed, one of the joys of life ; but that faultless melody, which drains into its harmonious flow all the rills of music hidden in spoken words, is but the sign and symbol of the life which it contains and reveals. When the young Goethe said, after reading Shakespeare for the first time, that he felt as if he had been reading the book of fate with the hurricane of life sweeping through it and tossing its leaves to and fro, he made it clear that he had read Shakespeare with his heart ; he had touched the vital power in the great dramatist, and he had been enriched for all time. Every great book is charged with life ; the measure of its greatness is the degree in which it has been vitalised by the great nature out of which it issued. This vital power is the heart and soul of the book, and to get at it and possess it is the highest task and the supreme reward of the reader of the book. When he has reached a point where, his intelligence alert and eager, he unconsciously absorbs the book, he has become co-operative with the writer, and, in a sense, on a level with him. It is to such readers that the great minds speak, and from such readers they hold back nothing they have learned of the mystery of life and art.

One may read the play of " Antony and Cleopatra " and get nothing from it but a series of brilliant pictures ; or one may read it and add a large measure of Eastern and Roman life to his own life, and push back the horizons of his own experience so as to include these great and tragical workings-out of human destiny under both eternal and historical conditions. Could a day of solitude and silence be given to a richer use than this? One will not drain the play of its meaning in many days, but one day set apart to it will make the work of succeeding days easy and inevitable. Here is a great piece of art, which is, like all kindred works, a great piece of life. To get at its secret one must use all intelligence, but above all one must open his heart to it ; one must be willing, first of all, to receive it fully and unresistingly ; there will be time enough for criticism later ; the first thing to be done is to possess the poem. When one forgets himself and surrenders himself to a work of art, he feels at the very start its obvious beauty; he gets the first intention of the poet ; he abandons himself to the music with which the thought first speaks to him, to the colour and form which instantly address the eye. He who would master a noble piece of art must begin with the purest, fullest, and simplest joy in its most obvious beauty.

This very beauty awakens the imagination, and now

the reader becomes a poet no less than the writer ; he
confirms the true art of the play by disclosing in himself the miracle which true art always works. For
great art is never complete in itself ; it is complete
only in the imagination of him who really sees it, and
when that imagination finishes the sublime work which
the greatest poet can only begin. And now Rome
and Egypt cease to be geographical expressions ; they
rise on the horizon of thought ; they are thronged
with hurrying feet, and life surges through their streets
and beats itself out against their walls. And that life
takes on its own form and atmosphere : Rome, massive, virile, masterful ; Egypt, languorous, voluptuous,
enervating. Cities, dress, atmosphere, are recreated ;
and, touched by the same spell, men and women whose
names were fading on the dusty page of history live
and move with a vitality which once made them
masters of the world-movements. These striking
persons reveal their several characters, disclose their
relations to the time, the institutions, and the his-
toric movement ; we are absorbed in their personal
destiny as it is wrought out against the background of
two civilisations. The story runs on with an ever-
widening sweep and with ever-clearing tendency, and
slowly, out of that which is personal and individual,
the vaster drama of the soul unfolds itself, and what
was Roman and Egyptian becomes universal and for
all time. When at last the curtain falls, we have made
conquest of a striking bit of history, of two diverse
kinds of civilisation, of one of the most splendid and

significant stories of human passion and suffering, and of a great chapter out of the spiritual story of the race. This appropriation has come to us, not by analysis, but by the co-operating activity of the imagination, opening the mind and the heart to the free play of the poet's purpose and genius; analysis may come later, but the vital quality and the spiritual secret of the play are mastered by unconscious receptivity. It is always better to give than to receive, and in giving ourselves we have gained Shakespeare.

THE POETRY OF FLAME.

ONE who has the passion for reading learns to read under all conditions; but there are books which refuse to compromise with the convenience of the reader, and demand not only the right moment but the harmonious atmosphere. One may read Dickens with impunity anywhere; the human interest in his stories is so close and so catholic that they gain rather than lose by the sense of the nearness and pressure of human life; but it would be little less than sacrilege to open Landor's "Hellenics" in a street-car, or Sir Philip Sidney's "Arcadia" on a ferry-boat. Books of this temper will not bear contact with the hard actualities of human condition; they exact the reverence of a quiet mood and an hour of solitude. So, I sometimes fancy, every book guards its innermost secret with certain conditions which, like the hedge of thorns about the sleeping Princess, preserve it for those elected by taste and temperament to master it. There are poems which need the high light of summer mornings out-of-doors; and there are poems which need the ruddy flame of the wood fire. All motion has a rhythm, if we are keen enough to detect it; and I suspect that every dancing flame playing capriciously

along the glowing logs has a music of its own. Sometimes, when one is in the mood, the rhythm of the fire
strikes into the rhythm of the verse, and the two flow
on together. Fortunate is the poet when Nature takes
up his song in her own key, and fortunate is the reader
when this special felicity befalls him !

An open fire finds its peculiar charm in the liberation of imagination which it effects. It is all colour,
motion, sound, and change, and he must be dull
indeed who does not straightway become a poet under
its spell. For the work of the fire is a symbol of the
work of the imagination ; it liberates the ethereal
qualities prisoned in the dense fibres of the wood ; it
transforms the prose of hard material into the poetry
of flame. Whether we respond to it or not, the hum
of the fire is a song out of the music to which all
things are set, and its brief burning is part of the
process by which, to those who see with the imagination, this hard, intractable world is always bearing that
harvest of poetry of which Emerson was thinking when
he wrote : "Shakespeare, Homer, Dante, Chaucer,
saw the splendour of meaning that plays over the visible
world ; knew that a tree has another use than for
apples, and corn another than for meal, and the ball of
the earth than for tillage and roads ; that these things
bore a second and finer harvest to the mind, being
emblems of its thoughts, and conveying in all their
natural history a certain mute commentary on human
life."

The open fire sings its song, heard or unheard, in

all ears. It is the oldest and most primitive of all the forms of service which men exact from nature ; but, glowing on all hearths and for all sorts and conditions of men, it is always and everywhere transforming the prose of life into poetry ; for poetry, being the soul of things, is universal. It is only the very highest gifts which, as Lowell has said of heaven, are to be had for the asking. To a few are given the shows of rank and the luxury of wealth, but purity, nobility, and self-sacrifice are to be had by every comer. We are all born poets, although so many of us defeat the purposes of nature. For the world produces poetry as naturally and inevitably as a tree bears its blossoms, and we are compelled to close our eyes to avoid seeing that which the imagination must see if it see at all. It is in what we call common things that poetry hides, and he who cannot find it there cannot find it anywhere. It is absence of the poetic mind, not lack of poetic material, which makes some periods so sterile in imaginative production. When the imagination is powerful and creative, everything turns to poetry, — the stranded ship on the bar, the rusty anchor at the wharf, the glimpse of cloud at the end of the street, the shout of children at play, the crumbling hut, the work-stained man returning from his task, — the whole movement and stir of life in the vast range of common incident and universal experience. Touch life anywhere with the imagination and it turns into gold, or into something less material and perishable. We live, move, and have our being in the atmosphere of poetry ; for every act of sacrifice, every touch of tenderness, every word of love, every birth of aspiration, is so much experience transformed into poetry. Could anything be more commonplace, to the mind that has not learned that the commonplace is always an illusion, than the fact that a young girl, living in rural solitude, had died? That was the bare fact, the prose rendering; and this is the truth, the poetic rendering : —

> "She dwelt among the untrodden ways
>   Beside the springs of Dove ;
> A maid whom there were none to praise,
>   And very few to love.
>
> "A violet by a mossy stone
>   Half hidden from the eye ! —
> Fair as a star, when only one
>   Is shining in the sky.
>
> "She lived unknown, and few could know
>   When Lucy ceased to be ;
> But she is in her grave, and, oh,
>   The difference to me !"

There is a kind of elemental simplicity of feeling, imagery, and diction in these brief lines that touches us like the ripple of a brook in the woods. Life has few facts more unadorned than those which furnish the material for these verses, but does the imagination flash its mysterious light anywhere in literature more distinctly? The little poem is as quiet, simple, solitary as the mountain tarn, but it is as deep ; and there are stars in its depths. It is an illusion that some things are commonplace, some experiences without significance, and some lives without vision and beauty. The wood becomes flame, the seed turns into flower, the mist athwart the rays of light is changed into the gold of the evening sky, the hidden and unconscious sacrifice flashes suddenly into one of those deeds which men count for proofs of immortality, the uncouth pleader of the frontier becomes the hero of the " Commemoration Ode," —

" New birth of our new soil, the first American."

THE FINALITIES OF EXPRESSION.

SOCRATES seems to most of us an eminently wholesome character, incapable of corrupting the youth, although adjudged guilty of that grave offence, and altogether a man to be trusted and honoured. And the tradition of Xantippe adds our sympathy to our faith. But Carlyle evidently distrusted Socrates, for he says of him, reproachfully, that he was " terribly at ease in Zion." It is quite certain that neither within Zion nor outside its walls was Carlyle at ease. No sweating smith ever groaned more at his task than did this greatest of modern English literary artists. He fairly grovelled in toil, bemoaning himself and smiting his fellow-man in sheer anguish of spirit ; producing his masterpieces to an accompaniment of passionate but unprofane curses on the conditions under which, and the task upon which, he worked. This, however, was the artisan, not the artist, side of the great writer ; it was the toil-worn, unrelenting Scotch conscience astride his art and riding it at times as Tam o' Shanter spurred his gray mare, Meg, on the ride to Kirk Alloway. Socrates, on the other hand, is always at ease and in repose. His touch on the highest themes is strong and sure, but light almost as air. There seem to be no effort about his morality, no self-consciousness in his piety, no strain in his philosophy. The man and his words are in perfect harmony, and both seem to be a natural flowering and fulfilment of the higher possibilities of life. Uncouth as he was in person, there was a strange and compelling beauty in this unconventional teacher; for the expression both of his character and of his thought was wholly in the field of art. He was an artist just as truly as Phidias or Pericles or Plato; one, that is, who gave the world not the processes but the results of labour; for grace, as George Macdonald somewhere says, is the result of forgotten toil. Socrates had his struggles, but what the world saw and heard was the final and harmonious achievement; it heard the finished speech, not the orator declaiming on the beach with pebbles in his mouth; it saw the completed picture, not the artist struggling with those obdurate patches of colour about which Hamerton tells us. When the supreme moment and experience came, Socrates was calm amid his weeping friends, and died with the quiet assurance of one to whom death was so entirely incidental that any special agitation would seem to exaggerate its importance; and exaggeration is intolerable in art.

This bit of vital illustration may suggest a deeper view of art than that which we habitually take, and a view which may make us for a moment conscious of the loss which modern life sustains in having lost so largely the art spirit. Men degenerate without a strong grasp on morality, but they grow deformed and unhappy without art. For art is as truly the final expression of perfect character as of perfect thought, and beauty is as much a quality of divinity as righteousness. When goodness gets beyond self-consciousness, when the love of man for God becomes as genuine and simple and instinctive as the love of a child for its father, both goodness and love become beautiful. Beauty is the final form of all pure activities, and truth and righteousness do not reach their perfect stage until they take on beauty. Struggle is heroic, and our imaginations are deeply moved by it, but struggle is only a means to an end, and to rest in it and glorify it is to exalt the process above the consummation. We need beauty just as truly as we need truth, for it is as much a part of our lives. A beautiful character, like a beautiful poem or statue, becomes a type or standard; it brings the ideal within our vision, and, while it fills us with a divine discontent, satisfies and consoles us. The finalities of character and of art restore our vision of the ends of life, and, by disclosing the surpassing and thrilling beauty of the final achievement, reconcile us to the toil and anguish which go before it. The men and women are few who would not gladly die if they might do one worthy thing perfectly.

The conscience of most English-speaking people has been trained in the direction of morality, but not in the direction of beauty. We hold ourselves with painful solicitude from all contact with that which cor-

rupts or defiles, but we are absolutely unscrupulous
when it comes to colour and form and proportion.　We
are studious not to offend the moral sense, but we
do not hesitate to abuse the æsthetic sense.　We fret
at political corruption, and at long intervals we give
ourselves the trouble of getting rid of it ; but we put
up public buildings which may well make higher intel-
ligences than ours shudder at such an uncovering of
our deformity.　We insist on decent compliance with
the law, but we ruthlessly despoil a beautiful landscape
and stain a fair sky, as if these acts were not flagrant
violations of the order of the universe.　The truth is,
our consciences are like our tastes ; they are only
half trained.　They operate directly and powerfully
on one side of our lives, and on the other they are
dumb and inactive.

An intelligent conscience insists on a whole life no
less than on a clean one ; it exacts obedience, not to
one set of laws, but to law ; it makes us as uncomfort-
able in the presence of a neglected opportunity as in
the presence of a misused one.　It is not surprising
that men are restless under present conditions ; there
is a squalor in many manufacturing and mining countries which eats into the soul, — an ugliness that hurts
the eye and makes the heart ache.　Blue sky and green
grass cry out at such profanation, and it is not strange
that the soul of the man who daily faces that hideous
deformity of God's fair world grows savage and that he
becomes a lawbreaker like his employer.　For lawbreak-
ing is contagious, and he who violates the wholesome

beauty of the world lets loose a spirit which will not discriminate between general and particular property, between the landscape and the private estates which compose it. The culprit who defaces a picture in a public gallery meets with condign punishment, but the man who defaces a lovely bit of nature, a living picture set in the frame of a golden day, goes unwhipped of justice; for we are as yet only partly educated, and civilization ends abruptly in more than one direction.

The absence of the corrective spirit of art is seen in the obtrusiveness of much of our morality and religion; we formulate and methodise so much that ought to be spontaneous and free. The natural key is never out of harmony with the purest strains of which the soul is capable, but we distrust it to such an extent that much of the expression of religious life is in an unnatural key. We are afraid of simple goodness, and are never satisfied until we have cramped it into some conventional form and substituted for the pure inspiration a well-contrived system of mechanism; for the Psalms we are always substituting the Catechism, and in all possible ways translating the deep and beautiful poetry of the spiritual life into the hard prose of ecclesiasticism and dogmatism. The perfect harmony of the life and truth of the divinest character known to men teaches a lesson which we have yet to learn. If the words of Christ and those of any catechism are set in contrast, the difference between the crudity of provisional statements and the divine perfection of the finalities of truth and life is at once apparent. We have learned in part the lesson of morality, but we have yet to learn the lesson of beauty. We have not learned it because in our moral education we have stopped short of perfection; for the purest and highest morality becomes a noble form of art.

ENJOYING ONE'S MIND.

WHO that lives in this busy, noisy age has not envied the lot of Gilbert White, watching with keen, quiet eyes the little world of Selborne for more than fifty uneventful years? To a mind so tranquil and a spirit so serene the comings and goings of the old domesticated turtle in the garden were more important than the debates in Parliament. The pulse of the world beat slowly in the secluded hamlet, and the roar of change and revolution beyond the Channel were only faintly echoed across the peaceful hills. The methodical observer had as much leisure as Nature herself, and could wait patiently on the moods of the seasons for those confidences which he always invited, but which he never forced; and there grew up a somewhat platonic but very loyal friendship between him and the beautiful rural world about him. How many days of happy observation were his, and with what a sense of leisure his discoveries were set down, in English as devoid of artifice or strain or the fever of haste as the calm movements of the seasons registered there! There was room for enjoyment in a life so quietly ordered; time for meditation and for getting acquainted with one's self.

Most of us use our minds as tools, which are never employed save in our working hours; we press them constantly to the limits of endurance, and often beyond. Instead of cultivating intimate friendship with them, we enslave them, and set them to tasks which blight their freshness and deplete their vitality. A mind cannot be always hard at work earning money for a man, and at the same time play the part of friend to him. Treated with respect and courtesy, there is no better servant than the mind; when this natural and loyal service is turned into drudgery, however, the servant makes no complaint and attempts no evasion, but the man loses one of the greatest and sweetest of all the resources of life. For there is no better fortune than to be on good terms with one's mind, and to live with it in unrestrained good-fellowship. We cannot escape living with it; even death is powerless to separate us; but, so far as pleasure is concerned, everything depends on the nature of the relation. The mind is ready to accept any degree of intimacy, but it is powerless to determine what that degree shall be ; it must do as it is bid, and is made a friend or a slave without any opportunity of choice.

To enjoy one's mind one must take time to become acquainted with it. Our deepest friendships are not affairs of the moment; they ripen slowly on the sunny side of the wall, and a good many seasons go to their perfect mellowness and sweetness. The man who wishes to get delight out of his mind, and be entertained by it, must give it time. The mind needs freedom and leisure, and cannot be its best without them. A good talker, who has a strain of imagination and sentiment in him, cannot be pushed into brilliant or persuasive fluency. If you are hurried and can give only partial attention, he is silent: the atmosphere does not warm his gift into life. The mind is even more sensitive to your mood and dependent on your attitude. If you are so absorbed in affairs that you can never give it anything better than your cast-off hours, do not expect gay companionship from it; for gayety involves a margin of vitality, an overflow of spirits. It is oftener on good terms with youth than with maturity, because young men drive it less and live with it more. They give it room for variety of interests and time for recreation, and it rewards them with charming vivacity. It craves leisure and ease of mood because these furnish the conditions under which it can become confidential; give it a summer day, and, if you have made it your friend, it will give you long hours of varied and wholesome entertainment. It has sentiment, imagination, wit, and memory at its command, and, like an Eastern magician, will transport you to any climate or bring any object to your feet. Never was there so willing a friend, nor one whose resources are so constantly ignored.

What a man finds in his mind and gets out of it depends very much on himself; for the mind fits its entertainment to the taste of its one tyrannical auditor. Probably few men have ever lived more loyally with their minds than Wordsworth. Fame found him a

recluse and left him solitary; crowds had no charms
for him, and at dinner-tables he had no gifts. He
was at his best pacing his garden walk and carrying on
that long colloquy with his mind which was his one
consuming passion. The critics speak of him as an
isolated, often as a cold, nature; but no man of his
time, not even Byron, put more passion into his work:
only his passion was not for persons, it was for ideas.
He had great moments with his mind, for he was
repaid for the intensity of his surrender of other occupations and interests by thrilling inspirations, — those
sudden liftings of the man into the clearness and
splendour of vision which the mind commands in its
highest moods. He who has felt that exaltation knows
not only what must have come often to Wordsworth
when the hills shone round him with a light beyond
that of the sun, but has touched the very highest bound
of human experience. A mind enriched by long contact with the best in thought and life, and cherished
by loving regard for its needs, often repays in a single
hour the devotion of a lifetime. Sometimes, beside
the lamp at evening, the book closes in the hand
because the mind swiftly flies from it to some distant
and splendid outlook; or, on the solitary walk, the
man stands still with beating heart because the mind
has suddenly disclosed another and diviner landscape
about him.

Wordsworth found imagination and sentiment in
his mind, as did the beautiful singer upon whom the
laurel next descended; but Charles Lamb had the

delights of wit. No men are on better terms with their minds than men of wit; one of the pleasures which they give their fellows of slower movement is the enjoyment which comes to them from their own unexpectedness. Most of us know what we shall think and say next ; or, if we do not know, we have no reason to anticipate either surprise or satisfaction from that part of the future which is to take its colour from our thoughts and words. A witty man, on the other hand, never knows what his mind will give him next; it is the unexpected which always happens in his mental history. Watch him as he talks, and note his delight in the tricks which his mind is playing upon him. He is as much in the dark as his auditors, and has as little inkling of the turn the talk will take next. His real antagonist is not the man who sends the ball back to him, but his own mind, which he is humourously prodding, and which is giving sharp thrusts in response. Charles Lamb found as much delight in his own quaintness as did any of his friends, and was as much surprised by those inimitable puns which stuttered themselves into speech as if they were being translated out of some wittier language than ours. It is pleasant to think of the suppressed fun that went on within him on the high seat at the India House. And Sydney Smith was another beneficiary of his own mind, whose way through life was so constantly enlivened by the gayest companionship that even the drowsy English pulpit of his time had little power to subdue his spirits or dull the edge of his wit. Who that has

talked with Dr. Holmes has not witnessed that charming catastrophe which befalls a man when his mind
runs away with him and dashes into all manner of
delightful but unsuspected roads, to bring back the
listener at last with a keen consciousness that there is a
good deal of undiscovered country about him, and that
he was a dull fellow not to have known it before. The
trouble is that he can never get himself run away with
in like fashion ! And yet most of us would be more
inspiring, more entertaining, and much wittier if we
gave ourselves a chance to get on terms of intimacy
with our own minds. Old Dyer had found, three
centuries ago, the delights of this fellowship when he
sang : —

> " My mind to me a kingdom is :
>   Such present joys therein I find,
> That it excels all other bliss
>   That earth affords or grows by kind ;
> Though much I want which most would have,
> Yet still my mind forbids to crave."

A NEGLECTED GIFT.

SYDNEY SMITH undoubtedly said aloud what a great many people were saying in an undertone when he called Macaulay " an instrument of social oppression." The brilliant historian and essayist had notable gifts, and has done much for the solace and entertainment of mankind ; but his memory must have had an appalling aspect for those who sat near him at a dinner-table. It was relentlessly accurate, and the boundaries of it seemed to fade out in an infinity of miscellaneous information. The man who knew his Popes so well that he could repeat them backward, stood in sore need of the grace of forgetfulness to save him from becoming a scourge to his kind. The glittering eye of the Ancient Mariner did not hold the wedding guest more mercilessly to his gruesome narrative than does a tyrannical memory bind the weary listener to the recital of things it cannot forget. Burton analysed Melancholy with great subtlety and particularity, but one wonders whether Burton's companionship would not have induced in another the very thing of which he tried to rid himself. Mr. Caxton was a dangerous person in his talking moods, as Pisistratus discovered at an early age, and needed to be diverted from themes which unlocked the stores of his knowledge.   For some men hold their information in great masses like the snow on the high Alps, and an unwary step will often bring down an avalanche.   Knowledge is of great moment and of lasting interest, but, like money, it must be used with tact and skill.   A good library has a solid foundation of books of reference ; but they are subordinate to a superstructure of art, grace, vitality, and truth.

If one had to choose between Macaulay, who never forgot anything, and Emerson, who rarely remembered anything in an exact, literal way, one would fasten upon the man of insight, and let the man of memory go his own way.   In these days the art of memorizing has had great attention, but the art of forgetting has no professed masters or teachers.   It is, nevertheless, one of the most important and charming of the arts ; the art of arts, indeed.   For the skill of the artist is in his ability to forget the non-essentials and to remember the essentials.   The faculty of forgetting gives the mind a true perspective, and shows past events in their just proportions and right relations.   The archæological painter forgets nothing, and his picture leaves us cold ; the poetic painter forgets everything, save the two or three significant things, and his picture sets our imagination aflame.   There is entertainment in old Burton, because the man sometimes gets the better of his memory ; there is inspiration in Emerson, because the man speaks habitually as if all things were new-created, and there were nothing to remember.   The past is a delightful friend if one can live without it, but to the man who lives in it there is no greater tyrant.

As the world grows older, the power to forget must grow with it, or mankind will bend, like Atlas, under a weight which will put movement out of the question. That only which illumines, enlarges, or cheers men ought to be remembered; everything else ought to be forgotten. The rose in bloom has no need of the calyx whose thorny shielding it has outgrown. When the recollection of the past stimulates and inspires, it has immense value; when its splendours make us content to rest on ancestral achievements, it is a sore hindrance. Filial piety holds the names of the fathers sacred; but we are living our lives, not theirs, and it is far more important that we should do brave and just deeds than that we should remember that others have done them. The burning of the Alexandrian Library was not without its compensations, and the rate at which books are now multiplied may some day compel such burnings at stated intervals, for the protection of an oppressed race. The books of power are always few and precious, and long life is decreed for them by reason of the very vitality which gives them their place; but the books of information must be subjected to a principle of selection, more and more rigorously applied as the years go by. Our posterity must conscientiously forget most of the books we have written.

For the characteristic of art — the thing that survives — is not memory, but insight. Our chief concern is to know ourselves, not our forbears; and to master

this modérn world, not the world of Cæsar or that of
Columbus. The great writer speaks out of a personal
contact with life, and while he may enrich his report
by apt and constant reference to the things that have
been, his authority rests on his own clarity of vision
and directness of insight. " Our age," says Emerson,
" is retrospective. It builds the sepulchres of the
fathers. It writes biographies, histories, and criticism.
The foregoing generations beheld God and nature face
to face ; we, through their eyes. Why should not we
also enjoy an original relation to the universe? Why
should not we have a poetry and philosophy of insight
and not tradition, and a religion by revelation to us, and
not the history of theirs? Embosomed for a season
in nature, whose floods of life stream around and
through us, and invite us, by the powers they supply,
to action proportioned to nature, why should we grope
among the dry bones of the past, or put the living generation into masquerade out of its faded wardrobe?
The sun shines to-day also. There is more wool and
flax in the fields. There are new lands, new men, new
thoughts. Let us demand our own works and laws
and worship."

Progress is largely conditioned on the ability to forget the views and conclusions which have become au-
thoritative. It took nearly a century of adventurous
sailing and perilous adventure to persuade Europe that
there was an undiscovered continent between India
and its own shores, — so possessed was the European
mind by the consistent blunders of the past about

this Western hemisphere. In the history of art, what are called the classical epochs — the periods of precision, accuracy, and conventional restraint — are inspired by memory; but the creative moments are moments of forgetfulness. The Renaissance was a moment of rediscovery, not of memory; the literary movement of this century involved a determined forgetting of the standards and methods of the last century. The age that lives in its memory of other times and men is always timid and imitative; the age that trusts its own insight is always audacious and creative. If we are to be ourselves, we must forget a good deal more than we remember.

There is a real grace of character in forgetting the things' that disturb the harmony of life. A keen remembrance of injustice or suffering breeds cynicism; the power to forget that we have been wronged, or that life has pressed heavily upon us, develops sweetness, ripeness, and harmonious strength. On the threshold of any future life, one must pass through a great wave of forgetfulness; it were better for us all if heaven were nearer to us by reason of the swift oblivion to which we consigned the wrongs we suffer in this brief burning of the candle of life.

CONCERNING CULTURE.

THERE are certain books which are touchstones of personal culture and taste, — books like Amiel's "Journal," Arnold's "Culture and Anarchy," Landor's "Hellenics," and Thackeray's "Henry Esmond," which involve a certain preparation of the mind for their reception and appreciation. For these books, and all books of their peculiar quality, contain an element of culture as well as of native gift; and a certain degree of culture must precede their appropriation by the reader. It used to be said that the odes of Horace were the special solace of gentlemen, — of men of a certain social training, which brought them into sympathetic contact with the worldly minded but charmingly trained poet of the Mantuan farm. There is a flavour as of old wine in many of the Horatian odes, and its delicacy is discerned only by the trained palate. In like manner the work of certain modern writers possesses a peculiar quality, impossible to define but readily detected, which finds its full recognition by, and discloses its entire charm to, minds which have had contact with the best in thought and life.

There was a time, fifteen or twenty years ago, when what is technically called culture was taken up by the

intellectually curious and the socially idle, and made a fad ; and, like all other fads, it became, for the time being, a thing abhorred of all serious-minded and sincere people. For a fad is always a sham, and a sham in the world of art or of literature is peculiarly offensive and repugnant ; it *is* the perversion, sometimes in the grossest form, of something essentially sound and noble. The ideal which took violent possession of so many people two decades ago was defective in that quality which is the very substance of genuine culture, the quality of ripeness. True culture involves a maturing of taste, intellect, and nature which comes only with time, tranquillity, and reposeful associations of the best sort. The more one really cares for it, the less he professes it ; the more one comes into possession of it, the less conscious does his pursuit of it become. It marks an advanced stage of a general maturing and ripening, and it discloses its presence in fulness of knowledge, easy command of resources, maturity and sureness of taste, and that sense of power which conveys the impression of a large and spontaneous force playing through a rich nature.

It is a mistake to suppose that this ripening of the man depends on a large acquaintance with books, although in these days, in most cases, books are indispensable aids. The Attic Greeks, the most genuinely cultivated people whom the world has yet known, had very slight contact with books ; but they had the faculty, due largely to the strain of poetry and hence

of imagination in their education, of getting the soul
out of life.   They discerned and appropriated, by a
training which had become instinctive, the best in life.
They chose the beautiful as readily and constantly as
we choose the inharmonious and the ugly ; they built
in harmony with the laws of art as uniformly as we
build in violation of those laws.   Their Parthenon
was as easy of accomplishment to them as the post-
offices of Boston, New York, and Chicago were to us.
They did not build better than they knew ; they built
because they knew, and their knowledge was due to
their culture.   That culture was based on life, not on
art, and hence their art had the compelling note of
an original utterance, and not the faint music of an
echo.

Shakespeare was a typical man of culture, whose
knowledge of a few books is beyond question, but
whose knowledge of many books is more than doubtful.   Oxford might have enriched him, as it did his
great contemporary Spenser, but he enriched himself
under circumstances apparently the most adverse.
There is no rawness in his thought, nor in his art; his
insight is not surer than his touch upon language.   In
every play there is the richness of substance, the fulness of thought, the easy hand upon all the keys of
speech, which betray the affluent nature, ripened beyond strength into sweetness.   Shakespeare was riper,
in some ways, than Goethe, whose whole life was
rigidly subordinated to the laws of growth.

This quality of ripeness, shared by Tennyson, Lowell,

Amiel, Arnold, is sometimes lacking in writers of great force and originality, and its absence always involves a certain impoverishment. If there is no obvious crudity, there is a certain thinness of tone, a rigidity of manner, a hardness of spirit. The ease, the grace, the charming unconsciousness, are absent ; one is continually aware of limitations, instead of being cheered and buoyed up by a sense of unexhausted power. Lowell gives his readers no greater delight than the impression, conveyed by every page of his writing, that he has not said half he has in mind. The landscape of thought, imagination, and knowledge through which he takes one, with a gait so easy and a humour so contagious, is full of variety and loveliness, but you are continually teased by vistas which hint at outlooks still more beautiful. What grace of bearing, modulation of tone, charm of manner, entire self-possession ! Here is no gifted and virile provincial who has broken away from hard conditions without rising above them, but a true man of the world of letters. This Olympian ease, which is the mark of the artist, is never the possession of the Titan, however strong.

It is culture which conveys this impression and confers this charm, and culture does not come by nature ; it does not come by work even, for strenuousness is the very thing it rids a man of; it comes of lying fallow and letting knowledge take possession of us. It is possible to know a great deal and be wholly without culture ; some scholars are as free from all trace of it as some well-conditioned men are of the charm of good-manners. Culture is knowledge become part of the soil of a man's life ; it is not knowledge piled up like so many pieces of wood. It is knowledge absorbed and transmuted by meditation into character. And this process involves leisure, solitude, the ability to keep one's hands and eyes idle at times. To get out of the current without losing its momentum is the problem of the man who wishes to be ripe as well as active. To possess one's mind, one must command a certain solitude and quiet; for there is deep truth in Goethe's saying that while character is formed in the stream of the world, talent is formed in quietness. That ripeness of nature which Americans are quick to notice in the best English writers, scholars, and thinkers is the result of a rich meditative strain running through lives of steadfast but unhasting industry. A bit of knowledge cannot enrich a man until he has brooded over it in the solitude of quiet hours. An Oxford man once said that the perfection of the lawns in the college gardens was only a matter of three or four centuries of rolling and cutting ; and the faces of some famous university writers and thinkers betray the long years rich, not only in study, but in meditation, — that quiet brooding over knowledge and experience which drains them of their significance and power for the lasting enrichment of our own natures.

THE MAGIC OF TALK.

THOSE who have the privilege of hearing really good talk know that it is the most delightful of all the resources which the fortunate man commands. A genuine talk, free, spontaneous, sincere, and full of intelligence, is always a thing to be remembered. It is a delight to the mind so keen as to be almost sensuous; but it is a joy which effects a certain liberation in those who share it. A talk is often the starting-point in a brilliant or commanding career. Everybody recalls Hazlitt's account of his earliest hours with Coleridge, and how the magic of that rare mind wrought upon him until it seemed as if he had broken into a new world. The originative impulse which makes a man conscious of his power and confident in it sometimes comes from a book, but oftener from a talk. For a talk has the great advantage over a book of bringing the whole man into play. There is a flow of individual force, a free outgoing of personal energy, in talk, which give not only the full weight of the thought, but the entire impetus of the man; and to listen to a rare man in full and free talk is not only to get the measure of his mind, but to feel the charm of his temperament; and temperament is half of genius.

There is an impression that writers put their best thought into books; but those who know the makers of books care, as a rule, more for the men than for the work they have done. There are, it is true, a few men from whom the gift of familiar and telling speech is withheld, and whose thought flows freely only from the point of the pen. Such men are so rare, however, that they confirm the almost universal possession of the genius for talk by men who hold genius in any other form. As a rule, the talk of men of letters is superior to their writing, and possesses a charm which their work fails to convey. A man of real strength is always greater than any specific putting forth of that strength; and the moments which make us aware of the general force give us also the adequate expression of the man's range and talent. Most men of rich and trained personality fail of complete expression in any formal way, and it is a common feeling among the friends of men whose writing attracts wide attention that it does not completely express the man. There was something in the force and directness of Tennyson's talk which did not make itself felt in his melodious verse; and, in spite of the poet's noble achievement, it is easy to understand the feeling of Fitzgerald that the Laureate never put his whole power forth. This was notably true of Lowell, whose opulence of intellectual resource and whose peculiarly rich and attractive personality gave his work, to many who knew the man, the air of brilliant improvisation rather than the final and masterful utterance of his affluent nature. Doubtless the friends of Shakespeare, the greatest of all improvisers, and apparently the most indifferent to the fate of his work, had a kindred feeling concerning the plays and poems of one whom his friends and earliest editors called " so worthy a friend and fellow," " whose wit can no more lie hid than it could be lost."

We shall never know what we have lost by the absence of a Boswell from the Mermaid Tavern on those evenings when Shakespeare, in those last rich years of his life, came up from Stratford and found in the fellowship of his old friends that solvent which gave his wit, his imagination, and his insight the liberation of a genial hour and company. Shakespeare's Boswell would probably have written the most deeply interesting book in all literature, — a pre-eminence of which Boswell's matchless account of Johnson comes within measurable distance. Johnson is, indeed, the foremost illustration of the general truth that men of letters are greater than their works. The author of " Rasselas " is very indifferently read in these days, but the great talker at the Literary Club and in the library at Streatham is probably the best-known figure of the last century. The writer was solemnly eloquent in that sonorous Latin style of his ; but the talker had a force and freshness which took by instinct to the sturdy Saxon side of the language. Great writing is never artificial, — a mode of speech which differs from the vernacular as a carefully planned lawn differs from the opulent carelessness of nature, — it is, rather, the inevitable form of expression to which a thought must ultimately come when it sinks into the consciousness of a race and become part of its deepest life. The supreme charm of talk lies in its unforced freshness and power; in the fact that the impulse takes a man unaware, and what is deepest and truest in him finds its way into speech.

The community of feeling which talk brings about sets the most sluggish fancy free, and solicits frankness from the most reticent. The greatest minds are not independent of their fellows; on the contrary, the measure of their greatness is accurately recorded in the extent of their obligations to others. A lyric poet may strike a few clear notes, as musical and as solitary as those of the hermit thrush hidden in the woods; but the rich, full music of the great dramatic poet draws its deep and victorious sweetness from the universal human experience, whose meaning it conveys and preserves. The touch of hand upon hand is not so real as the touch of mind upon mind; and as the contact of the hands gives a sense of sympathy and fellowship, so does the contact of mind give a sense of kinship of thought. To be alone is to be silent; to be with others is to express that which silence has brought us. Companionship of the right kind not only draws our hidden thought from its seclusion, but invites new thoughts to give it welcome and keep it company. The first half-hour may find the circle about the fire still somewhat constrained and slow of tongue ; for we people of English speech do not give ourselves freely to others ; but the second half-hour sees everybody intent and alert. There is a contagious quality in the air, and every man craves his moment of speech.   When talk gets down to the solid ground of entire truth and sincerity in those who share it, a capitalisation of knowledge is speedily and informally effected.   There lies in each mind a piece of information, and in every memory a bit of experience, which are freely contributed to the general fund.

The thought-product or result is, however, but a small part of the total outcome of a genuine talk ; under such a spell men speak their minds freely, but they also reveal themselves.   There is a gift of personal quality which is more rare than the gift of thought.   The thought of a great nature is precious, but the way in which it approaches the thought, and the significance it attaches to it, are still more valuable. Shakespeare was repeating a commonplace when he said, " We are such stuff as dreams are made of," but the commonplace became suddenly luminous and beautiful in a setting which turned its alloy into pure gold of insight and poetry.   The mystery and sublimity of life were familiar ideas when they took possession of Carlyle's imagination, but they returned from it flaming with an awful splendour which men had well-nigh forgotten.   That which is really rare in a man is not his thought, but himself; and it is this self, so hidden, so reticent, so marvellous, that somehow escapes from him in talk. When one thinks of Lowell, he does not recall " The Cathedral," but some hour before the fire, or some ramble over the hills, when the man behind the work somehow escaped from all association with it, and took on all the magic of a new acquaintance, added to the steadfast power of an old friend ; and of Emerson it is pre-eminently true that no one could really know him who had not come under the spell of his singular and indescribable personality. " Emerson's oration," wrote Lowell to a friend in 1867, "was more disjointed than usual, even with him. It began nowhere and ended everywhere, and yet, as always with that divine man, it left you feeling that something beautiful had passed that way, — something more beautiful than anything else, like the rising and setting of stars. . . . He boggled, he lost his place, he had to put on his glasses ; but it was as if a creature from some fairer world had lost his way in our fogs, and it was our fault, not his." His works have a quality like light, and a purity as of snows caught in the high Alps ; but the man was still clearer and rarer, — a nature not to be reflected in print, however skilfully ordered. It is this by-play of personality which gives talk a charm beyond all other forms of uttered speech. The literature one hears sometimes seems so much richer than the literature one reads that there comes with the rarest privilege regret that so much wealth is being spent on a few. Nature is always prodigal, however, and the supreme function of life is to produce great natures rather than great books. There is, moreover, a great hope hidden in this lavish indifference to the particular work and this steady emphasis on the superiority of the worker.

WORK AND ART.

THE most mysterious and irritating quality in a work
of art is the impression of ease which it conveys; it
seems to have been a piece of play; we cannot asso-
ciate work with it. Its charm lies in its detachment
from this workaday world, and its suggestion of intimacy with some other world where the most perfect
things are done with a prodigal easefulness. Nobody
ever happened upon Nature in her working hours;
apparently she is always at leisure. There is an illusion, however, in this apparent ease, which owes its
power of deception to our limitations. As a matter of
fact, Nature is never at rest; she is always at work;
but her work is so instinctive, so entirely within the
range of her force, so perfectly expressive of the energy
behind it, that it is, in the deepest sense, play. There
is no compulsion behind it, no shrinking from it, no
strain in it; it is quiet, easeful, normal, and adequate.
The artist finds Nature a teacher in this as in other
matters, and learns that the eternal charm of beauty
lies in its complete severance from all trace of work.
It is a bit of pure delight which comes to us from the
few lines in which the lyric poet, with winning simplicity, records an impression or confides an experience,

or from the few inches of canvas on which the artist preserves a swift glance at the landscape growing vague and mysterious in the twilight. The faintest odor of the lamp would empty the lines of their magic ; a hint of toil would destroy the illusion of a power behind the picture similar in kind, however inferior in degree, to that behind the landscape.

Behind every bit of genuine art there lies a training, always arduous, sometimes rigorous to the point of pain. There is no greater popular fallacy than the impression that men of letters and artists of all kinds are men of leisure. They are, on the contrary, men whose work never ends, and whose mastery is not only secured, but sustained, at immense cost of time, strength, thought, emotion, and will. The grace which banishes the thought of toil was bought at a great price ; it is a flower whose roots have often been watered by tears. Its perfection lies in its effacement of the " painful steps and slow " by which it has been reached ; so that its highest success involves the complete forgetfulness of the toil behind. The artist whose touch on the keys has a magical ease which revives our childhood's faith in the world of the " Arabian Nights " is a heroic worker, who pays for his success a price from which most men of affairs would shrink back appalled. The writer whose hand rests so lightly on the strings of speech, and makes them sing or thunder with such indifferent ease, knows that " torment of style " which pursued Flaubert all his days, — that painful pursuit of free, sincere, and noble expression, which is so constantly baffled, and so rarely touches the elusive goal. Two thousand and more sketches give a faint idea of the herculean toil behind Michel Angelo's "Last Judgment."

From this toil genius is no more exempt than talent; for perfection never comes by instinct; it is always the final expression of a perfectly harmonised nature. Shakespeare had his years of apprenticeship not less necessary and arduous than those of Gray; and Millet paid a great price for that marvellous skill of his. The first task laid upon the artist — the submission to the law of work when his mind is fomenting with all manner of spontaneous impulses — is so hard that art is allied forever to morality by the self-discipline which it involves; but the second task — the obliteration of every evidence of toil — is still more difficult. It is at this point that the artist reveals himself. He sets out with a goodly company, eager for that training which guards the gates of artistic achievement; but he is wellnigh deserted when he passes on into the next stage and begins to work with a free hand. Many men can work with sustained and noble energy, but very few men can transform work into play by coming to do instinctively, and with the ease of almost unconscious mastery, that which they began to do with deliberation and intention. In art it is pre-eminently and painfully true that many are called but few are chosen; and there is something pathetic, almost tragic, in the painstaking and tireless toil which is always climbing but which never plucks the flower of ease. For this reason

there is a great gulf set between the amateur and the
artist which is never crossed; for the artist is the servant of toil that he may become the master of his craft,
while the amateur, by evading the service, forever for-
feits the mastery. It is this last gift of ease that evidences genius and shows that the workman has become
a magician, — one who knows how to make the flower
bloom without the aid of botany, and the stars shine
without invoking astronomy. He who once did things
as work now does them as play, and, therefore, in the
creative spirit and with the creative force and simplicity.
When he was an apprentice he could explain his
methods, but now that he is a master the thing he does
with consummate skill and with such a touch of finality
is as much a mystery to him as to others; it is no
longer a contrivance, it is the deep and beautiful
product of his whole nature working together with that
mysterious force that resides in a rich personality.

There is something baffling in the quality of these
final touches in art. Why should these few lines on
paper, this bit of marble, this little group of verses,
stand apart from the toiling world as if they belonged
to another order of life and had their affinities with the
things that grow and bloom rather than with those that
are made and perish in the making? Why should a
civilisation fade out of human memory, and the delicate
vase or the fragile lyric survive? The answer to these
questions is found in Alfred de Musset's deep saying,
" It takes a great deal of life to make a little art." In
this vast workshop of life, with its dust and sweat and

4

din, it is the worker that is perfected oftener than the work ; and when some bit of perfection emerges from the dust and turmoil, it not only explains and justifies the toil behind it, but takes on a beauty which is half a prophecy.

A civilisation is not lost if, beyond the mysterious training of men which it silently effects, it leaves behind a few final touches, strokes, and songs as a bequest to that art which, by its very perfection, is the visible evidence of immortality. For when the worker so masters his material that skill is no longer mechanical but vital, no longer wholly calculated but largely instinctive, he becomes the instrument of a genius greater than his, and the channel of a truth deeper than any he has compassed. He escapes the limitations of the artisan and gains the freedom of the artist — to whom finality of expression is as natural as the gush of song from the wood or the glow of light in the east. For the highest form of all things is beauty; and art, in that deep sense which allies it with the spontaneity, the ease, the grace, and the play of nature, is the finality for which all toil prepares and in which all work ends. It takes centuries to make the soil, and then, born of earth and nurtured by the sky, blooms the flower, without care or toil, mysterious and inexplicable, — the touch of the imperishable beauty resting for an hour on its fragile petals.

JOY IN LIFE.

BROWNING'S "Saul" is one of those superb outbursts of poetic force which have for modern ears, accustomed to overmuch smooth, careful, and uninspired versification, not only the charm of beauty and energy in high degree, but of contrast as well. It sweeps along, eager, impetuous, resistless as the streams which descend the Alps and rush seaward with the joy of mountain torrents. So much contemporary verse is dainty, melodious, and unimpassioned that the tumultuous music of a virile song, overflowing all the shallow channels of artifice, and sweeping into the deep courses of human experience and emotion, is as thrilling as a glimpse of the sea after long hours on some pretty lake in some well-ordered park. Great art of any kind involves a great temperament even more than great intellect; since the essence of art is never intellectual, but always the complete expression of the whole nature. A great temperament is a rarer gift than a great mind; and it is the distinctive gift of the artist. Browning had the vitality, the freshness of feeling, the eagerness of interest, the energy of spirit, which witness this temperament. He had an intense joy in life simply as life, in nature simply as nature, without reference to what lay behind. For one must feel freshly and powerfully through the senses before one can represent the inner meaning of life and nature in art. In "Saul" there are elements of profound psychologic interest, but first and foremost there is the intense and vivid consciousness of the glory of life for a healthy human being, and of the splendour of the world. Rarely has this superb health found such thrilling expression as on the lips of the young poet beguiling the furious spirit in the mighty Saul : —

"Oh, our manhood's prime vigour ! no spirit feels waste,
´ Not a muscle is stopped in its playing nor sinew unbraced.
 Oh, the wild joys of living ! the leaping from rock up to rock,
 The strong rending of boughs from the fir-tree, the cool
        silver shock
 Of the plunge in a pool's living water, the hunt of the bear,
 And the sultriness showing the lion is couched in his lair.
 And the meal, the rich dates yellowed over with gold-dust
        divine,
 And the locust-flesh steeped in the pitcher, the full draught
        wine,
 And the sleep in the dried river-channel where bulrushes tell
 That the water was wont to go warbling so softly and well.
 How good is man's life, the mere living ! how fit to employ
 All the heart and the soul and the senses forever in joy ! "

After the wailing monotones and the chorus of lamentation which of late years have risen in .so many quarters, such music as this song of David's thrills the blood like a bugle-call ; and such a victorious strain was the natural prelude to the great vision of faith in which the song rises to its noble climax.

.

Brilliancy of temperament and the freshness and spontaneity of feeling which go with it are a part of the inheritance of such men as Gautier, whose virile face, with its great shock of yellow hair, had at times a leonine aspect ; but one hardly anticipates the possession of such gifts by a sick and overburdened man like Richard Jefferies, who was so long in finding his field, and who, when it was found, had so short a working-day in it. This temperament is, however, in a way, independent of physical condition; it is much more the buoyancy of a rich nature than the surplusage of a strong physique. In his last years Jefferies rivalled Heine in the intensity of his sufferings, but to the very end he answered the appeal of nature to the senses with passionate longing. In such men vitality triumphs over all moods and asserts the sovereignty of life even while life is swiftly receding from them. Few men have known the black shadows on the landscape more intimately than Jefferies, and rarely have these shadows been reflected with more appalling realism than in some of his pages. " Our bodies," he says, " are full of unsuspected flaws, handed down, it may be, for thousands of years, and it is of these that we die, and not of natural decay. . . . The truth is, we die through our ancestors; we are murdered by our ancestors. Their dead hands stretch forth from the tomb and drag us down to their mouldering bones." All the horror of Ibsen's " Ghosts " is condensed in that last sentence ; it falls on the ear like the sudden clang of the bell on the ear of the man waiting for the guillotine.

And yet Jefferies, being a really noble artist in the force of his feeling for nature and his power of recording her phenomena and reflecting her moods, had the deep, natural joyousness and the invincible vitality of the artistic temperament. He was sensitive to those gradations of colour and form of which the less gifted observer takes no account. " Colour and form and light," he says, " are as magic to me; it is a trance; it requires a language of ideas to express it. . . . A fagot, the outline of a leaf, low tints without reflecting power, strike the eye as a bell the ear. To me they are intensely clear, and the clearer the greater the pleasure. It is often too great, for it takes me away from solid pursuits merely to receive the impression, as water is still to receive the trees." With this quick impressionability there goes a passionate love of life and a passionate longing to have it flowing through him like a tide instead of ebbing with an ever-feebler current. In that heart-breaking book, "The Story of My Heart," this longing breaks from him in an anguish of unsatisfied desire : —

" There, alone, I went down to the sea. I stood where the foam came to my feet, and looked out over the sunlit waters. The great earth bearing the richness of the harvest, and its hills golden with corn, was at my back; its strength and firmness under me. The great sun shone above, the wide sea was before me, the wind came sweet and strong from the waves. The life of the earth and the sea, the glow of the sun, filled me; I touched the surge with my hand, I lifted my face to the sun, I opened my lips to the wind. I prayed aloud in the roar of the waves — my soul was strong as the sea, and prayed with the sea's might. Give me fulness of life like to the sea and sun, and to the earth and the air; give me fulness of physical life, mind equal and beyond their fulness; give me a greatness and perfection of soul higher than all things; give me my inexpressible desire which swells in me like a tide — give it to me with all the force of the sea!"

To some people this outcry for abundance of life and the joy of the senses may seem like a pagan mood; but if it be, it is a form of paganism sadly needed in these days of depression and debility. One would better be a frank and healthy pagan than a diseased and wailing pessimist; for paganism had its faith, its ideals, and its glorious productiveness, while a despairing melancholy has nothing but its own morbid self-consciousness. A return to the right kind of paganism might deliver us from some of the evils which have ensnared us. But the essence of the longing for the joy of the senses and for fulness of life, expressed in so many ways by so many men of artistic nature, is not sensuousness but vitality; it is the hunger of the whole nature for a deeper draught at the fountain whence its being flows; and its presence in the artist temperament explains its presence in great art. For the great art of the world is instinct with vitality; it overflows with life; it is full of joy and strength. Touching, as it does so constantly, the tragic themes, it is not mastered by them, but interprets them in the light of those higher laws whose servants we are. Shakespeare turns away from no tragic situation, and shrinks from no tragic problem ; but how serene he is, and what marvellous freshness of feeling shines through his work and gives it the touch of that Nature whose dews fall with every eve, and whose flowers bloom afresh with every dawn !

THE REAL AND THE SHAM.

THERE is, perhaps, no better test of mastership in any kind of artistic work than the effacement of the method by which the result is secured. A true work of art can never be taken apart; it is a living whole, and, although much may be said about it by way of analysis or of criticism, it is impossible to explain how it was put together. The same distinction exists between pedantry and culture; the trail of the pedant can be followed through his library back to the point from which he set out; he never for an instant gets off the beaten path. The man of culture, on the other hand, suggests his methods of personal training and enrichment no more than he suggests the air he breathes. He is so ripe in tone, so easily in command of his resources, and so sure of his tenure that there is no touch of professionalism about him. His personality is so rich and so interesting that one forgets that he is a writer or a painter or an orator. Mr. Booth found genuine pleasure in Mr. Sargent's striking portrait because it is free from all suggestion of the stage; it is the portrait of a man, not of an actor. And Mr. Booth was a charming example of a great artist devoid of the atmosphere of professionalism.

His talk touched naturally on incidents and themes which appealed to him by reason of his profession, and often lingered about experiences which had been part of his arduous and brilliant career; but it was the talk of a man of distinct individuality and force, not of an actor fitted into the grooves of a profession and moulded entirely to its uses.

The phrase " man of letters " is a happy one, because it emphasises the individual quality rather than the form of its expression; because it brings the man rather than the profession before us. One of the signs of mastery in art is freedom from mannerisms, from professional methods of securing effects. The finest orators have no set manner; the most inspiring preachers are free from the clerical habit and air; the greatest writers are the most difficult to imitate, because they offer the fewest obvious peculiarities. The real man of letters is always a man primarily, and a writer secondarily. His fingers are not blackened with ink, and his talk is devoid of that kind of pedantry which is never happy unless its theme is the latest book.

The love of literature is one of the noblest of human passions, but it has many degrees, and it is, unfortunately, easily imitated. There are a good many men and women who take up literary subjects and interests as they take up the latest fashions, — putting them on, so to speak, as they put on garments of the latest cut. There are so-called literary circles as devoid of true feeling for literature as the untutored tourist, restlessly rushing through art galleries with his Baedeker in his hand, is devoid of any real insight into art or love for it. Writers of force and originality are often slow in coming to their own, and are sometimes suddenly discovered by the many, long after they have been well known to the few; but the waves of interest in particular writers which sweep over society are a hollow mockery of any real and genuine knowledge. To rush wildly with the maddened throng after Browning for one short winter, to be diverted the next season by Ibsen, is to carefully destroy all hope of coming into real contact with either of these writers. A real love of art is shy of crowds, and wary of too close contact with "circles;" it does not protest too much; it hates, above all things, that pretentious use of technical phrases and that putting forward of the latest "discovery" which so often pass as literary conversation.

The spread of a sincere, unobtrusive, and teachable interest in books and other forms of art among the people of this country is a thing to recognise and rejoice in wherever it appears. It is not the crudity of undeveloped interest which is to be dreaded, but the crudity of sham interest; and the sham element is to be detected by its simulation of that which it does not possess. It is pretentious, and therefore it is essentially vulgar. It mistakes talk about books for that kind of conversation which is supposed to go on among literary folk; it dwells long and lovingly on personal contact with second and third rate authors; its test of literary quality is the professional air and manner. It gathers its small verse-writers, whom it profanely calls poets, listens to their smooth and hollow lines, applauds, drinks its tea, and goes home in the happy faith that it has poured another libation at the shrine of art. There is just now, and there probably will be for some time to come, a great deal of this sham love of literature in society; it is to be hoped that a sounder culture will some day make an end of it.

For the real love of books, like the real genius to write them, cometh not by observation; its roots are in the soul, and, being a part of a man's deepest nature, it is shy of any expression that departs a hair's line from absolute sincerity and simplicity. It detests the signs and insignia of professionalism; it shrinks from exploitation; it resents the profanation of that publicity which fastens on the manner in which the thing is done rather than on its aim and spirit. The world is prone to love wonders; it cares much more for the miracle than for the power which the miracle discloses, or the truth which it reveals. It has been in every age the anguish of the worker of wonders that he was sought as a magician rather than as a revealer of the mystery of life; and it is the prevalence of this spirit which makes the man of real artistic spirit so often indifferent to contemporary praise.

The simplicity and sincerity of a great man of letters have rarely been more clearly or attractively revealed than in the recently published correspondence of Sir Walter Scott. The enormous productivity of the great novelist was conditioned on long and arduous work; it would seem as if a man who was pouring out, through so many years, an unbroken stream of narrative would have become, in interest and habit no less than in occupation, a story-writer and nothing but a story-writer. But this is precisely what Scott did not become. The smell of ink is never upon his garments; he seems to care for everything under the Scotch heavens except books. Professionalism never gets the better of him, and he goes on to the tragical but noble end telling stories like a true-hearted man rather than like a trained *raconteur*. Other and lesser men may squander body and soul for a few new sensations, a little addition to literary capital; Scott remains sane, simple, and wholesome to the last day. One can imagine his scorn of literary fads, and of those who follow them; for literature was to him, not a matter of phrases and mannerisms and social conventions, — it was as simple, as native, and as much of out-of-doors as the Highlands whose secrets he discovered. There is a fine unconsciousness of any special gifts or calling in his letters; he writes about himself, as about all other things, in a natural key. Upon the appearance of "St. Ronan's Well," in 1824, Lady Abercorn tells him how greatly the book has affected her. "I like the whole book," she says; "it, like all the rest of those novels, makes one feel at home, and a party concerned. . . . Everybody reads these novels, and talks of them quite as much as the people do in England. . . . People are still curious as ever to find out the Author." And the

"Author," at the flood-tide of the most magnificent popular success in the history of English literature, replies at length, touching upon the novels in a purely objective and semi-humourous spirit, and then goes on to talk about his boy Charles, who is soon to leave for Oxford; about his "black-eyed lassie," who is "dancing away merrily;" about his nephew Walter, and about many other personal and every-day matters which touch the man, but which have nothing to do with the writing of books. The soundness of the Waverley Novels comes from the soundness of the simple, brave, true-hearted Sir Walter.

"My dear," he said to Lockhart, as he lay dying that September day; "my dear, be a good man." There is a tonic quality in such unconsciousness on the part of a man so opulent in some of the finest literary gifts, — a man of childlike nature, who drew his wonderful stories from the hills rather than from his libraries.; who was not shaken by the storm of popularity which burst upon him, nor dismayed by the disaster which threw its shadow like a vast eclipse on his magical prosperity; a great writer, who was first and always a man. It is well to seek refuge in such a great career from the passing fashions of the hour, from the exaggerations of unintelligent and capricious praise of commonplace men, and from that idle following of art which has as little veracity and reality in it as the rush and huzza of the crowd about the local statesman returned to his ward after a brief foreign tour.

LIGHTNESS OF TOUCH.

ONE of the happiest evidences that work has become play, and the strenuous temper of the artisan has given place to the artist's ease of mood, is that peculiar lightness of touch which is so elusive, so difficult, and yet so full of the ultimate charm of art. Does not Professor J. R. Seeley miss the point when he says: "Literature is perhaps at best a compromise between truth and fancy, between seriousness and trifling. It cannot do without something of popularity, and yet the writer who thinks much of popularity is unfaithful to his mission; on the other hand, he who leans too heavily upon literature breaks through it into science or into practical business"? He is speaking of Goethe, who sometimes leans so heavily on his art that he breaks through into philosophy, and whose verse, in didactic moods, comes perilously near prose; but is his general statement of the matter adequate or accurate? There is, it is true, literature so light in treatment and so unsubstantial in thought that it is distinctly trifling. "The Rape of the Lock," for instance, is in one sense a trifle, but as a trifle it is so perfect that it betrays a strong and steady hand behind it. Professor Seeley does not, however, limit the application of his statement; he evidently means to suggest that there is an element of trifling in literature as an art, for he puts it in antithesis with seriousness. Is there not an imperfect idea of art involved in this statement, and does not Professor Seeley confuse the ease and grace of literature with trifling?

There is, especially among English-speaking peoples, a lack of the artistic instinct, nowhere more discernible than in the inability to take art itself seriously, and in the tendency to impute to it a lack which inheres not in art itself, but in the perception of the critic. Moral seriousness is a very noble quality, but it is by no means the only form of seriousness. It may even be suspected that there is something beyond it, — a seriousness less strenuous, and therefore less obvious, but a seriousness more fundamental because more reposeful, and sustained by a wider range of relationships. Strain and stress have a dramatic as well as a moral interest, and often quite obscure those silent and unobtrusive victories which are won, not without sore struggle, but without dust and tumult. There are few things so deceptive as the lightness of touch which evidences the presence of the highest art; it means that the man is doing creatively what he once did mechanically. It is the very highest form of seriousness, because it has forgotten that it is serious; it has passed through self-consciousness into that unconscious mood in which a man does the noblest and most beautiful things of which he is capable, without taking thought that they are noble or beautiful. In the unfolding of character, where moral

aims are most distinct and moral processes most constant, there must come a time when a man is genuine
and sound, as nature is fruitful, by the law of his own
being. He passes beyond the stage when he needs
to say to himself every hour and with intensest self-
consciousness, " I must do right;" it becomes his
habit to do right.

Lightness of touch is not based on lack of seriousness; it is, rather, the product of a seriousness which
no longer obtrudes itself, because it has served its
purpose. Shakespeare was not less serious when he
wrote the exquisite calendar of flowers in " The
Winter's Tale" than when he drew the portrait of
Hector, but he was a greater artist; he had mastered
his material more completely; he had touched the
ultimate goal of his art. His touch is infinitely lighter
in " The Tempest," where his imagination plays with
the freedom and ease of a natural force, than in
" Troilus and Cressida," where he more than once
leans too heavily on poetry and breaks through into
philosophy. The philosophy is extremely interesting,
but it is not poetry; it rather illustrates the difference
between the strenuous and the artistic mood, and
throws a clear light on the process of evolution by
which the heavy touch is transformed into that light,
sure, self-effacing touch which gives us the thing to be
expressed without any consciousness of the manner of
the expression.

Milton's voice has great compass and his manner
great nobleness in " Paradise Lost," but the purest

5

and therefore the best poetry that came from his hand is to be found in "L'Allegro," "Il Penseroso," "Lycidas," the masque of "Comus," and the fragments of the "Arcades." These tender and beautiful lyrics, in which nobility of idea and ease of manner are so perfectly blended, were the products of the poet's most harmonious hours, when he was not less a Puritan because he was so much more the poet; when his mood was not less serious, but his relation to his time had less of self-consciousness in it; when he touched the deepest themes with consummate grace and lightness.

Goethe is at his best when his touch is lightest, and at his worst when it is heaviest. His lyrics are unsurpassed in that magical ease whose secret is known only to the masters of verse; he is as spontaneous, unforced, and fresh as a mountain rivulet. In his letters to Schiller he emphasises the dependence of the poet on the unconscious, creative mood. When this mood possesses him, the didactic tendency disappears, and the glowing spirit of poetry shines in song, ballad, and lyrical romance; he is all fire, grace, and lightness. But when the spontaneous mood forsakes him, and he writes by force of his training and skill, how slow and heavy is his flight, how cold and obvious his touch! He is nowhere more in earnest than in these inimitable songs, and has nowhere else a touch so devoid of manner, so instinct with grace and freedom.

The lightness of touch which charms us in literature

is not trifling; it is mastery. Whoever possesses it has gotten the better of his materials and of himself, and has brought both into subjection to that creative mood which pours itself out in finalities and perfections of speech and form as naturally as the vitality of a plant bursts into a flower which is both obviously and inexplicably beautiful. Whenever we come upon lightness of touch, we are in contact with a work of art; whenever we miss it, the work that lacks it may be noble, worthy, full of evidences of genius, but it is not a work of supreme artistic excellence.

THE POETS' CORNER.

ON dark days, when the fire sings its merry song in the teeth of sullen winds, the poets' corner is a place of refuge. There the great singers stand, row upon row, a silent but immortal choir; and the serene face of Emerson hangs on the little space of wall beside them. In the glorious company are those who sang the first notes in the earliest dawn of history, and those whose voices are just rising above the turmoil of to-day. What a vast movement of life have they set to music, and how many generations have they stirred to heroism or charmed into forgetfulness! There have been great teachers, but none so persuasive as these; there have been great leaders, but none so inspiring as these. I have often envied the Athenian boy sans grammar, sans arithmetic, sans reading-books, sans science primer; with no text-book but his Homer, but with Homer stored in his memory and locked in his heart. To be educated on the myths — those rich, deep interpretations of life — and upon the heroic history of one's race; to have constantly before the imagination, not isolated incidents and unrelated facts, but noble figures and splendid achievements; to breathe the atmosphere of a religion interwoven with the story of one's race, and to approach all this at the feet of a great poet — were ever children more fortunate? And when it comes to results, was ever educational system so fruitful as that which in the little city of Athens, in the brief period of a century and a half, produced a group of men whose superiority as soldiers, statesmen, poets, orators, architects, sculptors, and philosophers seems somehow to have been secured without effort, so perfectly is the spirit of their achievements expressed in the forms which they took on? The superiority of that training lay in its recognition of the imagination, and in its appeal, not to the intellect alone, but to the whole nature. We have great need of science, and science has been a grave and wise teacher, but the heart of life and the meaning of it belong to poetry; for poetry, as Wordsworth says, is "the impassioned expression which is in the face of all science." Science gives us the face, but poetry gives us the countenance — which is the soul irradiating its mask and revealing itself.

Upon all those who "cannot heare the Plannet-like Musick of Poetrie," Sir Philip Sidney, a poet in deed as in word, called down the direful curse, "in the behalfe of all Poets," "that while you live, you live in love, and never get favour for lacking skill of a Sonnet; and when you die, your memory die from the earth for want of an Epitaph." The range of that curse is more limited than appears at first sight, for while it is true that many of us have never listened to the children of the Muses, those of us are few who are not in

some way poets. We call ourselves practical, and imagine, in our ignorance, that there is a certain superiority in thus separating ourselves from the idealists,
the dreamers, the singers. But Nature is wiser than
we, and suffers us to apply these belittling epithets to
ourselves, but all the time keeps us in contact with the
living streams of poetry. The instant our nobler in·
stincts are appealed to, and we cease to be traffickers
and become fathers, mothers, children, lovers, patriots,
we become poets. To get away from poetry one must
begin by emptying the universe of God ; to rid life of
poetry one must end by following the hint of the great
pessimist and persuading men to commit universal sui-
cide. While the days come to us with such radiancy
of dawn, and depart from us with such splendour of
eve ; while flowers bloom, and birds sing, and winds
sport with clouds ; while mountains hold their sublime
silence against the horizon, and the sea sings its end-
less monotone ; while hope, faith, and love teach their
great lessons, and win us to work, sacrifice, purity, and
devotion, — we shall be poets in spite of ourselves and
whether we know it or not. There is no choice about
the matter; there is a divine compulsion in it; we
must be poets because we are immortal.

But there is a great difference between being or
doing something by compulsion, and being or doing
something by choice. They only get the joy of poetry
who love it and make fellowship with it. The richest
poetry must always be that which lies in one's soul, in
its deep and silent communion with nature and with

life ; but this unuttered and, in a true sense, unutterable poetry, becomes more definite and available as a resource if we make intimate friends with the masters of poetical expression. Shakespeare saw more of life than falls to the lot of all save his greatest readers; perhaps no one has yet brought to his pages the same degree of force and veracity of insight which are to be found in them. To read Shakespeare, therefore, is, for the greatest no less than for the least, a resource of the noblest kind; it is an interpretation of life through the imagination ; a disclosure of what lies in its depths, to be revealed only when those depths are stirred by the tempests of passion, or by some searching experience. A recent writer says that Shakespeare is to mankind at large what a man of perfect vision would be in a world of half-blind persons, — people who saw nothing clearly or accurately. Shakespeare does not describe an imaginary race and a visionary world ; he describes men as they are, and the world as it is ; the sense of unreality in his work, if one has it, comes from one's own limitations of sight. In other words, it is not the so-called practical mind which sees things as they are, but the mind of imaginative force and poetic insight. We move about in a world half realised, full of dim figures, vague outlines, hazy vistas ; Shakespeare lived in a world which lay in clear light, and which he searched through and through with those marvellous glances of his. Who has read English history with such an eye as the greatest of English poets? Hume recites the facts about Henry V. in an orderly and careful manner, but Shakespeare looks into the soul of the robust and virile king, and makes us see, not the trappings and insignia of power, but the interior source of that authority which flung the English yeomen like a foaming wave over the walls of Harfleur. The diamond is none the less in the quartz because we fail to see it, and the heroic and tragic possibilities are not lacking in hosts of human lives which seem entirely commonplace to most of us. That which makes some ages so much more inspiring and productive than others is not so much a difference in the material at hand as in the skill and power with which the possibilities of that material are discerned and turned to account; men do not differ so much in the possession of opportunities as in the clearness of sight to discern them and the force to make the most of them. This world can never be commonplace save to the dull and unseeing; and life can never be devoid of tragic interest save to those who fail to recognise the elements at work in every community and in every individual soul.

The men of poetic mind have many gifts, but none so rare and of such moment to their fellows as this clearness of vision. To really see clearly into the soul of things is one of the rarest of gifts, and it is the characteristic gift of the poetic imagination. That second harvest of which Emerson speaks is reaped only by the sickle of the imagination; to the common vision it does not even exist. This round world is distinctly visible to the dullest mind; but to such a mind the beauty, wonder, and mystery in which its secret lies hidden, are as if they were not. Men walk through life almost without consciousness of the daily miracle performed under their eyes; they become so familiar with their surroundings that they lose the sense of awe and wonder which flows from the clear perception of the fathomless sea of force in which all things are borne onward. One may drop his plummet in the nearest pool, and, behold, it also is fathomless. Every path leads into the presence of that infinite power to which we give different names, but which is the one great and eternal reality behind these apparitions of to-day. Now, of this unseen but sublime presence the imagination keeps us continually conscious; and the great poetic minds, in prose and verse, — in Plato's "Dialogues" and in Dante's "Divine Comedy," — fulfil their highest office in seeing and compelling us to see the spirit behind the form, the soul within the body. In the records which the imagination has kept in the art of the world are written the true story of the soul of man, the authentic history of his life on earth. And the charm of this revelation lies in its freshness, its variety, and its beauty. It does not preserve the past after the manner of the historians by pressing it like dried and faded flowers between the leaves of massive quartos; it preserves the very vitality which flowered centuries ago. The one supreme quality by which it lives is its marvellous life, — that life which keeps Ulysses still sailing the ancient seas, and Romeo still young and beautiful with the passion which, in spite of its own short life, is the evidence of immortality.

THE JOY OF THE MOMENT.

THE first warm spring days stir something like resentment against those ascetic and monastic ideas which for so many centuries set men at odds with nature, and almost broke the bonds between them. There is a delight in life which is often called pagan, so grossly has Christianity been misread. This delight, born of the pure joy of the mind in recognising the beauty of the world and its own inalienable share in it, is quite as much a duty as the most definite moral obligation ; but a long education will be needed before the real meaning of beauty is discerned, and the harmony between man and nature, shattered by Latin mediævalism, is restored. Meantime, fortunate are they to whom the bloom of the world is a never-ending joy, and who are able to snatch this unforced delight in an age when so few things are sought spontaneously, and so many are striven for with a strenuousness which defeats itself.

There was a great deal of Christianity in Paganism, if one goes to the New Testament for his ideals ; and there is, accordingly, a great deal of Paganism coming out in Christianity. The world is as beautiful as it was before the shadow of a divisive thought of himself made man a stranger in the house built for him with a splendour fit for immortal spirits; and the alien begins once more to find himself at home under the kindly stars and amid the ministrations of the seasons. There are few things which the modern world needs more than the power to take the joy of the moment, without that blighting afterthought which scatters every rose in barren analysis, and flings every fragment of gold into the crucible. The first use of the world is to see it, and get the delight which comes from the vision; but there are hosts of men so bent upon understanding how things are made that they pull them to pieces before they have really looked at them. One longs at times for the mood of the myth-makers, who often mis-read the facts, but who had a rare faculty of getting at the truth, and who had the joy of seeing the world as a great living whole, overflowing with beauty and divinity. There were greater things to learn in nature than some of the Greek poets saw; but they had a true instinct for getting into intimate relations with nature, and they knew how to enrich themselves with the loveliness which encircled them in sky and sea and woodland. There is a charm in Theocritus, for instance, with which the dawning summer puts one in renewed fellowship; a charm which seems to disclose a new reality when the advancing season becomes its comment and illus-tration. That charm resides in an immense capacity for enjoyment; in the power of surrendering one's self to the moment so completely that one slips the bonds of consciousness and loses himself in the flowing life of the world.   When one has, so to speak, shed himself, he is in the way of some of the rarest joys which mortal lips ever taste — joys as pure and sweet as any that are yielded to the highest moods.   " The unconsciousness of the child," says Froebel, " is rest in God," — a very deep and beautiful saying, which we shall do well to lay to heart.   Too many of us are under the delusion that nothing counts save activity, and that to rest in nature at times is to commit the sin of slothfulness.

The herdsmen whom Theocritus has immortalised were not always models of conscious rectitude, but they are often models of unconscious enjoyment. They note the seasons by a thousand delicate signs, and they mark the hours by a registry of time more sensitive than that on any dial.   The sky, the clouds, the sea, have perpetual interest for them ; and birds, leaves, winds, and flowers so mingle with their thoughts and occupations that the inward and the outward happenings seem all of a piece.   Nature has share in every moment, and divides her fruits and charms as if there were a secret contract between the fruit-bearer and the fruit-taker ; between the brook and the figure that bends over it ; between the sloping hillside and the herdsman who feeds his flock on the grass creeping close to the olive-trees.

> " Thyrsis, let honey and the honeycomb
>   Fill thy sweet mouth, and figs of Ægilus :
>   For ne'er cicala trilled so sweet a song.
>   Here is the cup ; mark, friend, how sweet it smells :
>   The Hours, thou 'lt say, have washed it in their well."

We have gone a long way in our real education when we have learned how to yield ourselves completely to the hour and the scene, for in this mood we learn secrets which defy our keenest scrutiny. Nature often has things to say to our silence which remain unspoken while we insist upon having speech with her. To sit at her feet is often more fruitful than to persist in putting our thought into her mind. Above all, to surrender ourselves to her mood is to feel her beauty with a keenness of delight which is like the adding of a new joy to life. To those who are preoccupied with their own thoughts a whole realm of happiness is as effectively closed as if it were walled and barred. To leave ourselves at home and go into the woods to find what is there, and not what we have brought there, is to come into a kingdom of God which, being without us, illuminates with a new and kindling light the kingdom within us. There are a delicacy of colour, a charm of changefulness, a swiftly shifting loveliness, which elude our hours of self-consciousness and reserve their enchantment for our moments of self-forgetfulness. As we open ourselves to these elusive influences, they not only silently steal into our souls, but they become more real and more constant. A new sense, or rather a new delicacy of sense, is born within us; we hear sounds which were inaudible before, and we see things that were invisible to our preoccupation.

And from this freshening of perception there comes not only a new joy in nature, but a new insight into

poetry. For the poets find their sphere in the observation and record of this more delicate and unobtrusive loveliness, and their power of beguiling us out of
ourselves lies in their faculty of finer vision. No truer
disclosure of this sensitiveness of spirit to the beauty of
the world has recently been made than that which
finds its record in William Watson's invocation to
" The First Skylark of Spring : " —

> " The springtime bubbled in his throat,
>   The sweet sky seemed not far above,
> And young and lovesome came the note ;
>   Ah, thine is Youth and Love.
>
> " Thou sing'st of what he knew of old,
>   And dreamlike from afar recalls ;
> In flashes of forgotten gold
>   An Orient glory falls.
>
> " And as he listens, one by one
>   Life's utmost splendours blaze more nigh :
> Less inaccessible the sun,
>   Less alien grows the sky.
>
> " For thou art native to the spheres,
>   And of the courts of heaven art free,
> And carriest to his temporal ears
>   News from eternity.
>
> " And lead'st him to the dizzy verge,
>   And lur'st him o'er the dazzling line,
> Where mortal and immortal merge,
>   And human dies divine."

THE LOWELL LETTERS.

It has long been the habit of many people to speak of letter-writing as a lost art, and to intimate that its disappearance is a phase of that deterioration of mind and manners which is constantly charged upon the spread of the democratic idea. Suits of armour having been relegated to the Tower, and the splendid dress of the Renaissance period no longer charming the eye save on festive occasions, the habit of exchanging confidences and opinions at length between friends has gone the way of all the earth! That there has been a change in the manner of letter-writing is beyond question, but that the change has been a deterioration is more than doubtful. When Mlle de Scudéry wrote "The Grand Cyrus," nothing short of the most stately figures, the most elaborate style, and a long row of volumes would suffice for a dignified romance; to-day we have some very humble people, some very simple speech, and a single volume of moderate size for the story of "Adam Bede." Will any one say, therefore, that the novel has lost dignity, power, or reality? In these days friends no longer constitute themselves reporters and news-gatherers, as in the

time when the news-letter, written over a cup of choco-
late in some London coffee-house, was the principal
means of communication between the metropolis and
the provinces. Changed conditions involve changed
methods and manners, but not necessarily worse ones.
French women have a genius and a training for social
life, for living together in a real and true way, from which
women of the English-speaking race are, as a rule,
debarred. Our strong and persistent sense of personality has certain fine rewards, but it costs a good deal
on the side of free and intimate relationship with others.
There are half a dozen groups of letters written by
French women which may be said to fix the standard
of this kind of writing; but those who know the France
of to-day intimately declare that this art was never
practised with more skill and charm than at this
moment.

However the case may be in France, it is certain
that this century has been peculiarly rich in this kind
of literature among English-speaking people, and some
of the very best modern writing in our language has
taken this form. When it comes to the question of
literary quality, there is nothing in letter-writing, from
the time of Howell down, more admirable than that
which makes every bit and fragment from Thackeray's
pen literature. In those estrays, to which he probably
attached no value, and to which in many cases he
certainly gave little time or thought, the touch of the
master is in every line, — that indefinable quality which
forever differentiates writing from literature. This

quality, which is personality plus the artistic power, is quite as likely to discover itself in the briefest note as in the most elaborate work; indeed, the careless ease with which a man often writes to his friend is more favourable to free and unconscious expression of himself than the essay or the novel over which he broods and upon which he works month after month, perhaps year after year. The suspicion of toil is fatal to a work of art, for the essence of art is ease; and for this reason the letters of some writers are distinctly the best things they have given us. Unfortunately, even letter-writers do not always escape the temptation to write with an eye to the future, and to put one's best foot forward, instead of opening one's mind and heart without care or consciousness.

Mr. Lowell's letters are not free from faults, but their faults spring from his conditions and temperament. and not from proximity to a large and admiring audience. The letters are simple, frank, and often charmingly affectionate; they reveal the heart of the man, and perhaps their best service to us is the impression they convey that the man and his work were of a piece, and that the fine idealism of the poet was but the expression of what was most real and significant to the man. The self-consciousness of the young Lowell comes out very strongly if one reads his letters in connection with those of the young Walter Scott; but it was a self-consciousness inherited with the Puritan temperament rather than developed in the individual nature. The strong, quiet, easy relations of Scott to his time and world are very suggestive of a power which has so far eluded our grasp, — a power which, could we grasp it, would make the production of great literature possible to us. Lowell had so many elements of greatness that one is often perplexed by the fact that, as a writer, with all his gifts, he somehow falls short of greatness. May it not be that all that stood between Lowell and those final stretches of achievement where the great immortal things are done was his self-consciousness? He was never quite free; he could never quite let himself go, so to speak, and let the elemental force sweep him wholly out of himself. But it is not probable that any one could have grown up in the New England of his boyhood and possessed this last gift of greatness. "I shall never be a poet," he wrote in 1865, "till I get out of the pulpit; and New England was all meeting-house when I was growing up." A generation later this unconsciousness had become possible, for Phillips Brooks possessed it in rare degree; it was the secret of that contagious quality which gave him such compelling power whenever he rose to speak.

Lowell's letters have the great charm of frankness, — a charm possessed only by natures of a high order. One is constantly struck with his simplicity, — that simplicity which is so often found in a nature at once strong and rich. Life consists, after all, in a very few things, and no one knows this so well as the man who has tried many things. There was in the heart of the old diplomatist the same hunger and thirst that were

in the heart of the young poet. Leslie Stephen says
of him : " He was one of those men of whom it might
be safely said, not that they were unspoiled by popularity and flattery, but that it was inconceivable that
they should be spoiled. He offered no assailable
point to temptation of that kind. For it is singularly
true of him, as I take it to be generally true of men
of the really poetical temperament, that the child in
him was never suppressed. He retained the most
transparent simplicity to the end."   And this comment
is delightfully confirmed by an incident reported by
the " Universal Eavesdropper : "   " Passing along the
Edgware Road with a friend two years ago, their eyes
were attracted by a sign with this inscription : ' Hospital for Incurable Children.' Turning to his com-
panion with that genial smile for which he is remarka-
ble, Lowell said quietly, ' There 's where they 'll send
me one of these days.' "   He professed not to know
of what Fountain of Youth he had drank, but he could
hardly have been ignorant that there was such a
fountain in his own nature. The " exhaustless fund
of inexperience " which he said was somewhere about
him was simply the richness of a nature which never
reached its limits and flowed back upon itself with that
silent but desolating reaction which sometimes gives
age a touch of tragedy.

The simplicity of Lowell's nature comes out also in
his dealing with ethical questions. He never sophisti-
cates, or perplexes himself or his readers with the
effort to justify the right and just thing by a train of

reasoning; he strikes straight at the heart of the matter.   Nothing seems to confuse him or to distort his
vision; he sees clearly, and what he sees he accepts
with childlike simplicity of faith.   This is the secret
of his singular effectiveness when he speaks on moral
questions.   There is an elemental rightness in his
view and an elemental authority in his voice.   Whether
he is dealing with the burning question of slavery, or
with the delusion of spiritualism, or with incorrupti-
bility in public life, or with honest payment of public
obligations, or with the right of property in books,
his perception flies like an arrow to its mark ; tradition,
custom, casuistry, not only do not confuse him — they
do not even reach him.   This quality of directness is
one of the most convincing evidences of greatness.
In a man of Lincoln's opportunities and experiences
its presence is not surprising, although none the less
admirable and rare ; but in a man of Lowell's culture
and wide contact with life it shines with a beauty made
more effective by the richness of the medium which it
masters.

" I love above all other reading the early letters of
men of genius.   In that struggling, hoping, confident
time, the world has not slipped in with its odious consciousness, its vulgar claim of confidantship between
them and their inspiration.   In reading these letters I
can recall my former self, full of an aspiration which
had not learned how hard the hills of life are to climb,
but thought rather to alight upon them from its winged
vantage-ground."   These words, called out by a gift

of " Keats's Life," are expressive of the feeling with which one dips into these letters written by the same hand, — letters full of disclosures of character ; of sidelights on a life of sustained dignity and fruitfulness ; of wit, humor, wisdom, and art.

THE TYRANNY OF BOOKS.

MR. LOWELL speaks of himself, in one of his most characteristic letters, as one of the last of the great readers, — a fortunate few who have had leisure and opportunity to stray at will through the whole field of literature. The true book-lover counts his easy intimacy with his library as a privilege beyond the purchasing power of money or fame, and would sooner part with all hope of share in either than with a resource which is a measureless delight. For the love of books becomes a passion in the end, and when the heart once falls a prey to this passion, most things that other men care for become dross. Great fortunes do not so much as touch the imagination that has kept company with Una and Rosalind; and the fret and fever of the rush for place have no power to mar the repose of the library in which the devout reader sits as in a shrine. To those who have become past-masters of the art of reading, the spell of the book is not to be resisted; but no description can convey an idea of its power to those who have not fallen under it. The real reader believes in his heart that every hour apart from his books is an hour lost; that all duties and necessities which draw him away are not only interruptions, but impertinences; and that the busy, restless, distracted world has no more right to disturb him in his devotions than had the marauding bands of mediæval warfare to break in upon the fugitives who had taken refuge in the sanctuaries. This is what the past-master of the art of reading believes in his heart; but he has kept good company too long to exalt his privilege at the expense of his fellows by making public confession of his faith.

We often need, however, to protect ourselves from our friends; for we cannot bring the best gifts to the service of friendship unless we guard the independence of our own thought and action against even the solicitation of affection. Lovelace struck a very deep note when he sang : —

> " I could not love thee, Dear, so much
> Loved I not Honour more."

A great affection is often a great peril, and a great passion brings with it a commensurate danger. The great reader is the most fortunate of men, but he is also one of the most sorely tempted; and his temptation is the more seductive because it comes in the guise of an opportunity. It seems a great waste of time, and a piece of very bad taste as well, to spend much time with one's own thought when the best thought of the world may be had for the opening of a volume close at hand. There is a kind of brazen effrontery in trying to think things out for ourselves when Plato's Dialogues let us into a world of thought

not only very noble in its structure, but enchanting in
its atmosphere.   In the long run, however, one would
better do without Plato than lose the habit of thinking.
And how shall a man justify serious and prolonged
observation of life when the plays of Shakespeare lie
on his table, to be opened in any hour, and never to
be closed without a fresh sense of the marvellous
searching of the heart and mind of man which has
made its registry on every page? No reader ever
gets to the bottom of Shakespeare's thought, and surely
it is folly to try to master life for ourselves when we
are unable to fully possess ourselves of this interpretation of it !   In like manner, Theocritus and Wordsworth and Burns make our efforts to establish personal
relations with nature seem at once intrusive and ridiculous.   Whichever way we turn we are confronted by
our betters, and the sensitive spirit feels abashed and
appalled in the presence of the masters who have
possessed themselves in advance of every field which
he wishes to explore.   The great reader, with so much
unappropriated material at hand, is tempted to become
a mere receptacle for knowledge or a mere taster of
the vintages of past years.

A good deal of originative force is absorbed in
enjoyment in the library, and many a man who might
have seen and said things for himself sees them only
through the eyes of others and says them only in their
language.   Activity, it is true, is often only a mischievous form of idleness, and it would be better if
some men were content to enjoy instead of striving to

create; much current writing brings this truth home
to us. Nevertheless, a man would better be himself
in a poor way than be somebody else in a very rich
way. The modest house which a man builds for himself, with his own brains and hands, is more creditable
to him than the great house which he occupies by the
grace or good-will of another. A man owes it to himself to stand in personal relations with life, and not to
touch it at second hand; and one would better see it
for himself than get report of it from the keenest
observer that ever studied it; one would better scrape
acquaintance with nature on any terms than get his
knowledge of her at second hand. The chief thing
for every man is to come into actual contact with the
things that make for his life; and for that contact no
price is too great, — not even the price of turning the
key in the library door and suffering the cobwebs to
cloud the titles of the books. The bookworm has an
enjoyment so keen that we must envy even while we
condemn it. But the pleasure costs too much. It
costs that which no man has a right to pay.

It involves, among other losses, a diminution of the
power of appreciation and appropriation; for the man
who is always and only a reader fails to get the last
flavour out of his pursuit. There is not only a great
freshening of the receptive sense by variation of occupation and experience, but there is also notable gain
in insight by supplementing the observation of others
with studies of our own. No man can fully enter into
the Shakespearean comment upon life until he has first

learned something of life at his own charges; and no man can feel the ultimate charm of Wordsworth and Burns who has not first plucked the daffodil and the daisy with his own hands. The men of many books are often impoverished so far as real wealth of thought, knowledge, and feeling is concerned, and the men of few books are often incalculably rich in these possessions. Burton loved his books well and not unwisely, but we read his pages of compacted quotation only at intervals and with great temperance; while of Shakespeare, the man of few books, and those few mainly translations, we can never get enough. It is true that there has been but one Shakespeare, and in any age the men are few who have any original comments to make. If life were chiefly a matter of expression, it would be better every way that a few should speak and that the rest of us should keep silence in the presence of our betters; but expression is the gift of the few, while experience, and the growth which comes through it, is a birthright which no man can sell without selling himself. Whether silent or speaking, a man must be himself, see with his own eyes, and work with his own hands. The crowd of glorious witnesses who look down upon his toil from the shelves of his library will not despise it because it is humble, nor will they scorn his achievement because it is meagre and imperfect. Their noblest service is to give us faith in ourselves and joy in our work.

THE SPELL OF STYLE.

THE reality of art is constantly affirmed by the sudden flaming of the imagination and the swift response of the emotions to its silent appeal. Whenever a real sentence is spoken on the stage, what a silence falls on the theatre! Something has gone home to every auditor, and the hush of recognition or expectancy is instantaneous. There is, perhaps, no scene in the modern lyrical drama which is more beautiful in its suggestiveness than that in which Siegfried strives to comprehend the song of the birds, and vainly shapes his stubborn reed to give them note for note. The light sifts down through the trees; the leaves sway gently in the currents of air, rising and falling as if touched by the ebb and flow of invisible tides; the sound of running water, cool, pellucid, unstained by human association, steals in among the murmurous tones; and in the midst of this mysterious stir of life sits Siegfried, pathetically eager to catch the keynote of a harmony whose existence he feels, but the significance of which escapes him. The baffling sense of a music just beyond our hearing continually besets us, and, like Siegfried, we are forever striving to master this mysterious melody.

There is in all artistic natures a conviction that a deep and universal accord exists between all created things, and that beyond all apparent discords there is an eternal harmony.   This fundamental unity philosophy is always searching for and art is always finding, and the thrill which runs through us when a perfect phrase falls on our ears, or a new glimpse of beauty passes before our eyes, is something more than the joy of the æsthetic sense ; it is the joy of the soul in a new disclosure of life itself.   There is a deep mystery in this matter of harmony and of its power over us : the mystery which hides the soul of life and art.   If we could penetrate that mystery we should master the secret of existence, and find truth and beauty, life and its final expression, so blended and fused that we could no more separate them than we can separate the form, the colour, and the fragrance of the flower ; for they have one root, and are but different manifestations of the same vital force.

The psychologists tell us that every man has a rhythm discoverable in his walk, gesture, voice, modulation, and sentences ; a rhythm which is the natural expression of the man when all the elements of his nature come into harmony, and the inner and outward, the spiritual and the physical, flow together in perfect unison.   At rare intervals such a man throws his spell over us with written or spoken words, and we are drawn out of ourselves and borne along by a music of speech which touches the senses as delicately and surely as it touches the soul.   Such a nature has passed beyond the secondary processes of the intellect into the region of ultimate truth, and speaks, not with the divisive tongue of the Scribe, but with the authority of Nature herself. For the power of the masters is a mystery even to themselves; it is a power so largely unconscious that the deepest knowledge its possessor has of it is the knowledge that at times he can command it, and at other times it eludes him.

" I know very well," says Lowell, " what the charm of mere words is. I know very well that our nerves of sensation adapt themselves, as the wood of the violin is said to do, to certain modulations, so that we receive them with a readier sympathy at every repetition. This is a part of the sweet charm of the classics." It is a part, indeed, but only a part; the spell is deeper and more lasting, for it is the spell which the vision of the whole has for him who has seen only a part; which a sudden glimpse of the eternal has for him whose sight rests on the temporal; which a disclosure of perfection has for him who lives and strives in a world of fragments. The tones of the violin get their resonance and fulness from the entire instrument, — from the body no less than from the strings; and the magical melody which a Paganini evokes from it is the harmony of a perfected violin. In like manner the magical spell lies within the empire of that man alone whose whole being has found its keynote and natural rhythm.

This lets us into the secret of style, — that elusive quality which forever separates the work of the artist from that of the artisan. For the final form which a great thought or a great emotion takes on is as far removed from accident, caprice, or choice as are the shape and colour of the flower; it was ordained before the foundations of the world, by the hand which made all life of a piece and decreed that the great things should grow by an interior law, instead of being fashioned by mechanical skill. Body, mind, and spirit are so blended in every work of art that they are not only inseparable, but form a living whole. Not only is the Kalevala, in idea, imagery, and words, a creation out of the soul of the race that fashioned it, but its metre was determined by the actual heart-beat and respiratory action of the men who, age after age, recited it from memory. Every original metre and all rhythm have their roots in the rhythmical action of the body; language, arrangement, and selection, in the rhythmical action of the mind; and emotion and passion, in the currents of the soul: so that every real poem is a growth of the entire life of a man; and the spell of its deep harmony of parts, as well as its melody of words, is compounded of his very substance.

This spell, which issues from all art, resides in no verbal sleight of hand, no tricks with phrases: it is a sudden flashing out of the perfection at the heart of things; and we are thrilled by it because in it we recognise what is deepest and divinest in our own natures. If this spell were at the command of any kind of dexterity, it would be sought and gained by a host of mechanical experts; but it is the despair of the dexterous and the strenuous : it is as elusive as the wind, and as completely beyond human control.   Nothing is more certain than that Shakespeare has a style ; he has a way of saying things so entirely his own that one is never at a loss to identify his phrase in any company ; indeed, it is not too much to say that if some stray line of his were to come to light, with no formal trace of authorship about it, the great poet would not be despoiled of his own for an hour.   And yet no one has ever imitated Shakespeare !   The Shakespearean idiom is absolutely incommunicable.   The secondary work of Milton has often been copied, — it is, indeed, easily imitated, for it is full of mannerisms ; but Shakespeare, in the processes of his spell-weaving, is no more to be overtaken than is the tide of life silently rising into leaf and flower.   At his best, Shakespeare is magical ; he is beyond analysis or imitation ; he has come into such touch with nature that the inner harmony, the ultimate music, becomes audible through him. When the real significance of style dawns upon us, it is not difficult to understand the spell which resides in this perfection of phrase, nor the eagerness with which men pursue it.   The true artist lives in the constant anticipation of seeing life as it is, and putting the vision into words that bring with them the power and harmony of that tremendous revelation.

THE SPEECH AS LITERATURE.

In the earlier days of the literary art, when life and its expression in speech were in closest relation, voice, gesture, and personality, revealed in face and bearing, were as much a part of literature as language itself. The Greek choral dance, which Mr. Moulton aptly calls "literary protoplasm," was the expression of the soul through all the forms at its command, — words, song, gesture, movement. The balladist and, later, the bard gave their recitations or chanting monologues an effective accompaniment of intonation, accent, emphasis, and gesture; and the result was, in some cases, literature, which was something more than words set in beautiful or impressive order.

In like manner, there has always been an oratory which was something more than spoken thought, which has had all the elements of art, and has been, therefore, to the men who came under its spell, spoken literature. The great mass of speaking is, necessarily, for the moment only; it has an immediate object; it is addressed to a special audience; it finds its inspiration in an occasion. Such speaking is often forcible, witty, eloquent, and effective; but it is not literature. It is distinctly ephemeral, and, having accomplished its purpose, it is forgotten, like all other tools and implements of construction. The oratory which is literature, on the other hand, touches great themes, allies itself with beauty or majesty of form, and, although addressed to an immediate and visible audience, makes its final appeal to that unseen but innumerable company who, in succeeding ages, gather silently about the great artists and are charmed and inspired by these unforgotten masters.

To this company of orators who made speech literature by dignity of theme, breadth of view, beauty of form, and harmony of delivery, George William Curtis belonged. He was not the greatest of those who, in this New World, have used the platform as a vantage-ground of leadership. He had not the organ-tones of Webster, nor the incisive style and matchless vocal skill of Phillips, nor the compass of Beecher; but in that fine harmony of theme, treatment, style, and personality which make the speech literature, he surpassed them all. Less effective for the moment than Phillips, his art has a finer fibre and a more enduring charm. When he spoke, it seemed as if one were present at the creation of a piece of literature. He saw his theme in such large relations, he touched it with a hand so true and so delicate, he phrased his thought with such lucid and winning refinement and skill, his bearing, enunciation, voice, and gesture were so harmonious, that what he said and his manner of saying it seemed all of a piece, and the product was a beautiful bit of art, — something incapable of entire preservation, and yet possessing the quality of the things that

7

endure. The enchantments of speech were his beyond any man of his generation, and he gave them a grace of manner which deepened and expanded their charm.

Perhaps the most obvious characteristic of Mr. Curtis's oratory was its harmony. There were no dissonances in it; there was none of that falling apart of thought and expression which so constantly mars the charm of public address. Thought, language, voice, and gesture flowed together, and ran at times like a shining stream, rippling into humour, breaking into musical cadences, but sweeping on with continuous and unbroken flow. Such speech was literature in a very high sense, because it was essentially art, — native force, a trained personality, and a sure and varied craftsmanship combining in a result which obliterated all trace of processes, and existed only as a complete expression of a high and noble nature. For there was no dissonance between Mr. Curtis's aims and spirit and his oratory. The fatal fluency which makes a man the characterless reflection of the mood and moment was utterly alien to him; he was free from that beguiling immorality to which so many men of easy speech fall a prey, — the immorality of high-flying rhetoric and low-flying thought and aim. He held himself above his gift, and turned all its possibilities of temptation into sources of power and influence. For he spoke out of a deep sincerity, and with a steadfastness of purpose which made his long public life one long integrity. There was a great personal peril in an optimism so persistently avowed, in an ideal of life so steadily held aloft in speech as splendid as itself, — the peril of making the speaker's life meagre and dwarfed in contrast with the richness and beauty of his art. But Mr. Curtis's life and his art were of a piece ; and, while his judgment was not free from the errors which beset all human judgment, no man can point to any severance between the image of life which he revealed to the souls of countless young men and the life he lived with tireless industry and unflagging energy to the day of his death.

The harmony which characterised his addresses was significant of the artistic quality which he possessed in very rare degree. It is true that his life ran very largely in ethical channels, and that he used the platform especially to influence the wills of his auditors and to inspire them to definite courses of action ; but even in dealing with moral questions he was preeminently an artist. Right thought and right action seemed to him essential to harmonious living ; and he was moved not so much by the wrong against which he spoke as by the ideal of symmetrical life which its very existence violated and jeopardised. He was long in the very thick of the bitterest controversy of the century, but there was always a finer note than that of antagonism in his pleas and arguments ; he touched the great chords of justice, freedom, and brotherhood. A reformer of a radical type, he always rose out of the atmosphere of agitation ; it was not destruction which he sought, — it was the demolition of the false construction, in order that the noble lines of the true structure might become as clear to others as they were to him. Whether he pleaded for the emancipation of the slave or the removal of the last vestige of restriction on the private and public action of women, he spoke always as one before whose eyes a great vision of the future shines, and in whose soul that vision has become an article of faith. It was completeness and harmony of life which he sought ; and while his ethical sense had a Puritan keenness and authority, it had also the wider vision and the broader relationships of one who sees life as a whole, and who sees it as a great harmony, whose final and eternal expression is beauty.

Art is so precious, and, in these later days, so rare and so difficult of possession, that it is hard to reconcile one's self to the disappearance of such an artist as Mr. Curtis. For, while the words which he spoke remain, the charm, the delicacy, the spell, can never be recalled ; they are a part of that spoken literature which has often calmed or stirred the hearts of men, but which perishes even in the moment of its flowering. And yet, in a deep sense, all art is imperishable ; for the goal of ultimate excellence can never be touched in any generation without imparting that deep and noble delight which is the swift recognition by every soul of its own ideals. When art comes back to us once more, in some riper and sweeter time, perhaps we shall care more for the delight of its birth than for its power to persist. When the streams run with brimming current, we are indifferent to the reservoirs ; our joy is not in the volume of water, but in the sweep and rush of the living tide.

A POET OF ASPIRATION.

THERE are few names in this century which have had, for young men especially, greater attractive power than that of Arthur Hugh Clough. This power has never been widely, but in many cases it has been deeply, felt. It has its source more in the nature of the man and in the conditions of his life than in his work, although the latter is full of the elevation, the aspiration, and the beauty of a very noble mind. But it is not as a finished artist, as a singer whose message is clear and whose note is resonant, that Clough attracts; it is rather as a child of his time, as one in whom the stir and change of the century were most distinctly reflected. There was an intense sympathy with his age in the heart of Clough, a sensitiveness to the tidal influences of thought and emotion, which made his impressionable nature, for a time at least, a prey to agitation and turmoil; and there is no more delicate registry of the tempestuous weather of the second quarter of the century than that which is found in his work.

It was in November, 1836, that Clough, a boy of seventeen, exchanged school life at Rugby for college life at Oxford. He had always been in advance of his opportunities; he had led each form successively; he was the best swimmer and the first runner in the school; he was so manly, genuine, and wholly lovable that when he left for Oxford every boy in the school waited to shake hands with him; his scholarly prominence was so marked that in his last year Dr. Arnold broke the silence which he invariably had preserved in awarding prizes, and publicly congratulated him on having secured every prize and won every honour which Rugby offered, and crowned his achievements by gaining the Balliol scholarship, then and now the highest honor open to the English school-boy. With such a record of fidelity and ability behind him, Clough entered upon his career at Oxford. He had not won the heart and enjoyed the teaching of Arnold without some comprehension of the largeness of thought and the noble intellectual sympathy which made his master the ideal teacher of his time; his mind was already playing, with a boy's eager and buoyant expectancy, about the problems of the age. He had learned already that loyalty to truth, whatever it costs and wherever it leads, is the only basis of a life of intellectual integrity. At Rugby he left one of the largest, freest, and most progressive minds of a generation rich in men of commanding ability; at Oxford he met those persuasive, subtle, and eloquent teachers who were to lead the greatest reactionary movement of the time. John Henry Newman, luminous in thought, fervent in spirit, winning in speech, was steadily draw-

ing away from modern life to the repose and authority
of the Middle Ages. The very air throbbed with the
stir of a conflict which drew all sensitive minds within
the circle of its agitation, and the eager expectancy
which filled the hearts of the leaders seemed to prom-
ise a new day of spiritual impulse and ecclesiastical
splendour. Then, if ever, was realised that beautiful
vision of Oxford which Dr. Arnold's son has given to
the world, when she lay "spreading her gardens to the
moonlight, and whispering from her towers the last
enchantments of the middle age."

Clough, in the fulness of his early intellectual
awakening, had already passed beyond the spell even
of an enchantment so alluring and magical as that
which Newman's eloquence was throwing around many
an eager spirit; he had gone too far on the road to a
free and noble mental life ever to turn back and sit
once more in the shadows that fell from cathedral
towers, and leave to others the guidance and direction
of his thought. But no young man could live in that
seething vortex and not be driven hither and thither
by the mere force of the currents of thought; for two
years, he says, "I was like a straw drawn up the
draught of a chimney." He had passed from the
influence of one of the freest to the influence of one
the most reactionary minds of the day, and the tumult
of conflicting opinion compelled him to examine and
re-examine questions the consideration of which belongs to maturer years. Amid the conflict which went
on about and within him, he carried himself with such

a steady resolution and with such a calmness of faith in the victory of truth that among his contemporaries he was soon felt as an independent force, preserving amid the agitation the quietude of soul which is the possession of the true thinker. Clough was not long overwhelmed and tossed helplessly from one side to the other of the whirling vortex of discussion; he was stimulated by the agitation into larger and freer play of mind upon the great questions of life, and he was filled — as an open mind cannot but be filled when all the elements are in motion — with the hope of a nobler world of faith some day to roll out of the cloud and darkness. In this eager expectancy, this pure and breathless aspiration, he may well stand in our thought for a whole group of men upon whom the questioning of this century has come, not to paralyse, but to inspire. Let him speak for himself : —

> " 'T is but the cloudy darkness dense ;
>   Though blank the tale it tells,
> No God, no Truth ! yet He, in sooth,
>   Within the sceptic darkness deep
> He dwells that none may see,
>   Till idol forms and idol thoughts
> Have passed and ceased to be :
>   No God, no Truth ! ah, though, in sooth,
> So stand the doctrine's half ;
>   On Egypt's track return not back,
> Nor own the Golden Calf.
>
> " Take better part, with manlier heart,
>   Thine adult spirit can ;
> No God, no Truth ! receive it ne'er —
>   Believe it ne'er — O man !
>
> .   .   .   .

No God, it saith ; ah, wait in faith
    God's self-completing plan ;
Receive it not, but leave it not,
    And wait it out, O man ! "

Defective as poetry, these verses express, nevertheless, the spirit and attitude of a free, religious nature,
and they have the charm of Clough's habitual veracity.
And where shall we find a truer expression of the
feeling which lies deepest in the heart of this century
than that contained in these striking verses : —

"Go from the East to the West, as the sun and the stars direct
    thee,
  Go with the girdle of man, go and encompass the earth.
  Not for the gain of the gold — for the getting, the hoarding,
    the having,
  But for the joy of the deed ; but for the Duty to do.
  Go with the spiritual life, the higher volition and action,
  With the great girdle of God, go and encompass the earth.

"Go ; say not in thy heart And what then were it accom-
    plished,
  Were the wild impulse allayed, what were the use or the
    good !
  Go, when the instinct is stilled, and when the deed is accom-
    plished,
  What thou hast done and shalt do shall be declared to thee
    then.
  Go with the sun and the stars, and yet evermore in thy spirit
  Say to thyself : It is good ; yet is there better than it.
  This that I see is not all, and this that I do is but little ;
  Nevertheless it is good, though there is better than it."

It is the spirit of youth which breathes in these
impressive lines and gives them a tonic quality. At a

time when so much diseased and cowardly thought finds its record in verse, it seems almost a duty to recall the large and hopeful utterance of a sane and healthy nature, in full sympathy with the time, and often in genuine anguish of spirit because of it, and yet serene and aspiring to the very end.

THE READING PUBLIC.

MR. HOWELLS, who is not only a prolific and successful writer, but a faithful custodian of the dignity of his craft, has recently said that publishers have their little superstitions and their "blind faith in the great god Chance." This worship of the uncertain deity is perhaps explained by the statement that —

"a book sells itself, or does not sell at all. . . . With the best or the worst will in the world, no publisher can force a book into acceptance. Advertising will not avail, and reviewing is notoriously futile. If the book does not strike the popular fancy, or deal with some universal interest, which need by no means be a profound or important one, the drums and the cymbals shall be beaten in vain. The book may be one of the best and wisest books in the world, but if it has not this sort of appeal in it, the readers of it, and worse yet, the purchasers, will remain few, though fit. The secret of this, like most other secrets of a rather ridiculous world, is in the awful keeping of fate, and we can hope to surprise it only by some lucky chance."

These are the words of a man who, by virtue of the quality of his work and the long-continued and close relations he has maintained with what is popularly

called the reading public in this country, has every
right to claim attention when he speaks on such a
subject. The publisher of largest experience is, as a
rule, freest to confess his inability to predict in advance the fate of a book by a new author, or, for that
matter, the fate of any particular book ; and this fact
seems to prove that there is in the business of offering
literary work to the public a large element of what, for
lack of a better name, the publisher calls luck or
chance.

And yet the mind rebels against the presence of
so unintelligent a factor as chance in the relation of
readers to literature ; for literature is not only the
greatest of arts, but stands in most intimate relations
with those who come under its influence, and there is
a certain profanation in the determination of such a
relation by the accident of a manner which fits the
mood of the moment, or of a style which captures the
wayward or idle fancy of the passing crowd. The
mind revolts against chance as a determining factor in
any field, but the persistency of its revolt in this particular field is evidenced by the constantly repeated
effort to secure trustworthy data regarding the relative
popularity of books. These efforts assume that there
are principles of taste or conditions of culture determining the choice of books, which may be discovered
if the data can be collected. Such attempts to ascer-
tain the tastes of the reading public are often, no
doubt, stimulated by curiosity ; but the subject is one
of prime importance, not only to the writer and the

publisher, but to the community at large; since there is no more decisive test of intelligence than the quality and character of the books most widely read.

In this country one great difficulty in dealing with the matter lies in the fact that there are, not one, but many, reading publics which are mutually exclusive of one another; for the public that concerns itself with Dante and Goethe, for instance, is not only indifferent to the productions of the cheap novelist, but is in blissful ignorance of the depressing fact that her productions are sold by the thousand at the news-stands. A homogeneous reading public does not exist, at this moment, in this country, although there is good reason to believe that we are on the way to form such a community. It may be that we shall not produce our greatest books until we have first secured, not only the possibility of a wide and representative appreciation of them, but that pressure for expression of deep and universal emotion and thought which fairly forces great books into being. The closest relation between the writer and the public which has ever existed produced, or at least recognised at the first glance, the most perfect literature the world has yet known. The Athenian writer of the great period was so intimate with his audience that his constant appeal was not to his own consciousness, but to theirs; and to every allusion in the play, the dramatist knew that the whole city, assembled about the stage, would instantly respond. Inaccuracy, false sentiment, or defective art could not survive the ordeal of a presentation so close and a hearing at once so swiftly appreciative and so relent-lessly critical. The Athenian audience did not read, it listened; and to the sensitive imagination of the writer there must have been a compelling power in the silent urgence of a craving for race-expression at once so intense and so exacting. Such an appeal could have come only from a constituency united by homo-geneous ideas, traditions, and intelligence. The chief value of this fact for us lies in the illustration which it offers of the normal, that is to say the highest, relation between writers and readers.

Among English-speaking people the existence of a reading public — a body of readers, that is, representa-tive of all classes — does not date farther back than the time of De Foe, whose "True-Born Englishman" was one of the first pieces of writing in our language to secure, by reason of its timely interest and its charac-teristic vigour, a national reading. The people who, a little later, found delight in the society of "The Spec-tator" were no small company, but they must have been, from the nature of those charming chapters of Addisonian comment and chronicle, a homogeneous group, sharing a certain degree of social opportunity and general culture. And this statement holds true of the constituency of the greater part of the writers of the last century, who, despite many differences of talent and method, held certain literary traditions in common, and rarely strayed beyond the horizon of the small world of cultivated people.

In this century, however, writers have come to deal

in the most direct and uncompromising manner with every form of human experience ; while, at the same time, the wide diffusion of elementary education and the ease with which books of every kind are set up, printed, bound, and offered for sale, have formed a large reading public without intellectual training, and have supplied this public with a mass of books devoid of all literary quality, and having nothing in common with literature save the outward aspect of page, type, and cover. The knowledge of good and evil in art, which can hardly be said to have come to the Athenian, so uniformly high was the quality of the work offered him, is possessed in fullest measure by the reading publics of to-day ; and it is this very fact which gives their choice of books its significance. For there is to-day, for the first time, entire freedom of choice ; there have been worthless books before, but they were never so numerous, so accessible, and so low in price as during the last twenty-five years. They are thrust upon us at every turn, at prices which bring them within reach of the meditative bootblack. When it was difficult to find publishers for worthless books, and necessary to sell them at prices which put them on the top shelf so far as the poorer people were concerned, there was, naturally, a very small publication of such books, and a still smaller constituency for them. It is well to remember, therefore, that the old audience of cultivated readers has not ceased to exist, — there is every reason to believe that it constantly grows larger, — but it is swallowed up in a vast assemblage of readers gathered from all classes in the community, and furnished with a practically unlimited supply of reading-matter of every kind. If our sins are more numerous than the sins of our fathers, let us do ourselves the justice to remember that our temptations are multiplied many fold; and that while they had to seek evil and pay for it, we must strive in all public conveyances to keep it out of our hands, at a price which, under the delusion of getting something for nothing, becomes a new temptation.

SANITY AND ART.

In reading Homer, Dante, Shakespeare, and Goethe, one is constantly impressed not only with the range and power of these great artists, but with their sanity and health. Their supreme authority in the realm of art resides as much in their clearness of vision as in their artistic quality; they were essentially sound and wholesome natures. They had the fresh perception, the true vision, the self-control, of health. The world was not distorted or overshadowed to them; they saw it as it was, and they reported it as they saw it. Health is, indeed, one of the great qualities of the highest art, because veracity of mind and of emotion depends largely upon health, and veracity lies at the base of all enduring art. To the reader of contemporary books Homer is the greatest of antiseptics; after so many records of diseased minds, so many confessions of morbid souls, the " Odyssey " is a whiff of air from the sea, borne into the suffocating midsummer atmosphere of a city street. To exchange Marie Bashkirtseff's " Journal " for the great epic of the sea is like coming out of some vaporous tropical swamp into the sweep of the ocean currents, free airs blowing from every quarter, and the whole stretch of sky visible from horizon to horizon. Mr. Higginson has somewhere told the story of an English scholar who gave his entire time to Homer, reading the "Iliad" three or four times every winter, and the "Odyssey" as many times every summer. There might be a certain contraction of interests in such a life, but there could hardly be any disease.

Vitality, the power to live deeply and richly, is perhaps the surest evidence of greatness; to be great, one must have compass and range of life. The glorious fulness of strength which prompts a man not to skirt the shore of the sea of experience, but to plunge into its depths, has something divine in it; it confirms our latent faith in the high origin and destiny of humanity. The ascetic saints, about whose pale brows the mediæval imagination saw the halo slowly form, were noble in self-sacrifice and heroic purity; but there will come a higher type of goodness, — the goodness which triumphs by inclusion, not by exclusion; by mastering and directing the physical impulses, the primitive forces, not by denying them. For the highest spiritual achievement is not for those who shun life, but for those who share it, and the sublimest victory is to him who meets all foes in the open field.

The first tumultuous outburst of vitality, often very unconventional in its manifestations, is not to be confused with vice, which is always and everywhere a kind of disease. "We are somewhat mad here, and play the devil's own game," wrote Goethe to Merck during that first wild winter at Weimar, when Wieland could find no epithet but *wüthig* to describe him, and the good Klopstock wrote his famous letter of expostulation and warning, and received his still more famous and stinging reply. No doubt the strong currents of life overflowed the normal barriers in those gay months when the Ilm blazed with torches at night and the masked skaters swept past to the strains of music, the Poet and his Duke leading the riot. But it was a festival of youth far more than an outbreak of vice, as the sternest censors soon saw'; and in that splendid vitality there was the prophecy of eighty-four years of unhasting and unresting energy.

The early letters of Scott have a delightful freshness and buoyancy born of the man's soundness of nature, — a soundness which was untouched by the mistakes and misfortunes of his later life ; and the perennial charm of the Waverley Novels resides very largely in their healthfulness. They take us entirely out of ourselves, and absorb us in the world of incident and action. If they are not always great as works of art, they are always great in that health of mind and soul which is elemental in all true living. Men cannot be too grateful for a mass of writing so genuine in tone, so free from morbid tendencies, so true to the fundamental ethics of living.

Disease is essentially repulsive to all healthy natures ; it is abnormal, and, although pathetically common, it is in a sense unnatural. It seems like a violation of the natural order ; and, in the long run it is, since it finds its cause or opportunity in the violation of some law of life. We never accustom ourselves to it, and we never cease to resent it as the intrusion of a foreign element into the normal development of life, and an interference with the free play of its forces. And our instinct is sound: disease is unnatural; it is a deflection from the normal line and order. Its victim is, for that reason, incompetent to report the facts of life correctly, or to reach trustworthy conclusions in regard to it.

Because it is a deflection from the line of health and a departure from the normal order, disease has rightly a deep and painful interest; it throws light on the conditions upon which health rests; but no physician studies disease to discover the normal action of the organs. And yet this is precisely what we have been doing during the last two centuries; for we have accepted in very large measure the conclusions of diseased natures regarding the significance, the character, and the value of life. We have suffered men of diseased minds to be our teachers, and, instead of looking up into the clear skies, or seeking the altitudes of the hills, or finding fellowship with strong, natural men in the normal vocations, we have waited in hospitals, and listened eagerly to the testimony of sick men touching matters about which they were incompetent to speak. We have suffered ourselves to become the victims of other men's morbid tendencies and distorted vision.

The men and women whose judgment of the nature and value of life has any authority are few; for the phenomena of life are manifold, and most men and women have neither the mental grasp, nor the range of knowledge, nor the breadth of experience requisite for a mastery of these phenomena. Other men and women are disqualified to pass judgment upon life because they are too constantly subject to moods to see clearly and to report accurately what they see; and a deep dispassionateness lies at the foundation of all adequate judgment of life. For obvious reasons, the testimony of the diseased mind is untrustworthy; it is often deeply interesting, but it has no authority. The "Journal" of Marie Bashkirtseff has a peculiar interest, a kind of uncanny fascination, because it is the confession of a human soul, and everything that reveals the human soul in any phase of experience is interesting; but as a criticism of life the "Journal" does not count. The novels of Guy de Maupassant have a great charm; they are full of a very high order of observation; they are skilful works of art; but they are misleading interpretations of life because they were the work of a man of diseased nature, — a man of distorted vision. Beauty of form does not always imply veracity of idea; and while beauty has its own claim upon us, the ideas which it clothes have no claim upon us unless they are the product of clear vision and sound judgment. It is one of the tragic facts of life that a thing may be beautiful and at the same time poisonous; but we do not take the poison because it comes in a beautiful form. We are too much the prey of invalidism; we give too much credence to hospital reports of life. We need more Homers and

Scotts, and fewer Rousseaus and Bashkirtseffs. We need to rid ourselves of the delusion that there is any distinction about disease, any rare and precious quality in morbid tastes, temperamental depression, and pessimism. The large, virile, healthful natures, who see things as they are, and rise above the mists and fogs of mood, are the only witnesses whose testimony about life is worth taking, for they are the only witnesses who know what life is.

MANNER AND MAN.

RUSKIN's declaration that when we stand before a great work of art we are conscious that we are in the presence, not of a great effort, but of a great power, touches the very heart of the artist's secret. For there is nothing so clear to the student of art in all its forms as the fact that its mysterious charm resides, not in any specific skill or gift, but in its quality, that subtle effluence of its inward nature. The loveliness of nature is sometimes so transcendent that the delight it conveys is akin to pain; it brings us so near the absolute beauty that a keen sense of separation and imperfection besets us. The still, lustrous evenings on the Mediterranean sometimes bring with them an almost overwhelming loneliness; they fill the imagination with the vision of a beauty not yet held in sure possession. About every work of art there is something baffling; we do not quite master it; we are not able to go with free foot where it leads. Nor are we able to explain the processes by which it receives and conveys its charm. If it were merely a great effort, we could discover its secret; but it is not a great effort, it is a great power.

Nothing that flows from a great work is so significant or so impressive as this impression of power, — of a great inward wealth in the nature of the artist which is inexhaustible. A hint of toil dispels the magic of a picture as certainly as the smell of the midnight lamp robs the written word of its charm, or the perception of calculated effects breaks the spell of oratory. The artist does not become an artist until craftsmanship has become so much a part of himself that it has ceased to have any abstract being to his thought; it has simply become his way of doing things, his manner of expression. There is nothing more significant of the reality and the finality of art than the searching tests which confront the man who endeavours to master it, — tests which protect it from the touch of all save the greatest, and preserve it inviolate from the contamination of low aims and vulgar tastes. Nothing is so absolutely secure as art; its integrity is inviolate because, by the law of its nature, it cannot be created save by those who comprehend and reverence it. It is as impossible to make art common or vulgar as to stain the heavens or rob the Jungfrau of its soft and winning majesty. It is easy to call commonplace or ignoble productions works of art, to exploit them and hold them before the world as types and standards of beauty; but popular ignorance is powerless to convey to a book or a picture that which it does not possess in itself. There is a brief confusion of ideas, a short-lived popularity, and then comes that final oblivion which awaits the common and the inferior masquerading in the guise of art. "The Heavenly Twins" and the "Yellow Aster" provoke wide comment, and alarm the timid who love real books and dread any cheapening of the noble art of literature; but there is no cause for alarm: these books of the moment, and all books of their kind, are separated from literature as obviously and as finally as the wax imitation from the flower that blooms, dewy, fragrant, and magically fresh, on the edges of the wood. What is called popular taste does not decide the question of the presence or absence of artistic quality; a work of art justifies itself; for its appeal is not to the taste of the moment, but to that instinct for beauty in the soul which sooner or later recognises the conformity of the human product to the divine reality. It is to the eternal element in men that the great work speaks, and its place is determined, not by capricious and changing tastes, but by its fidelity to that absolute beauty of which every touch of art is the revelation. The ignorance of a generation may pass by the masterful works of Rembrandt, but the question of the greatness and authority of "The Night-Watch" and "The Gilder" was never for a moment in the hands of the artist's contemporaries or successors; it was in Rembrandt's hands alone. Taste changes, but beauty is absolute and eternal.

The law which bases the power to produce art, not upon external skill, but upon the nature of the artist, not only protects it forever from pretenders and tricksters, but allies it to what is deepest and greatest in the life of the world. The magic of Shakespeare's style is not more wonderful than the veracity of his thought. The old proverb, "Manners maketh man," was never more clearly verified than in the case of this noble artist, whose style is at once so unmistakable and so literally inimitable. Those who have not learned the interior relation of style to soul, and who do not clearly see that style is not an element in literature, but literature itself, will do well to meditate on " The Tempest," or even on " The Two Gentlemen of Verona." For in Shakespeare at his best we have that identification of the artist with life, that absorption of knowledge into personality, that realisation of the eternal unity between truth of idea and beauty of form, which mark the perfection of art. In the finest Shakespearean dramas we are never conscious of effort; we are always conscious of power. The knowledge, the manner, and the man are one; there is perfect assimilation of the outward world by the inward spirit; idea and expression are so harmonious that the form is but the flowering of the soul. When observation has passed into meditation, and meditation has transformed knowledge into truth, and the brooding imagination has incorporated truth into the nature of the artist, then comes the creative moment, and the outward form grows not only out of the heart of the thought, but out of the soul of the man. Shakespeare is full of these magical transformations by which knowledge becomes power, and power passes on into beauty; and in these transformations the mystery and the processes of art are hidden but not wholly concealed.

THE OUTING OF THE SOUL.

THE gospel of personal righteousness finds many voices; the gospel of a full and rich life, fed from all the divine sources of truth, beauty, and power, still needs advocates. The old atheism which shut God out of a large part of his world still lingers like those drifts of snow that, in secluded places, elude the genial sun. Men are as slow to learn the divinity of nature as they have been to learn the divinity of humanity; as slow to accept the revelation of nature as to accept that of the human soul. It is difficult to realise how completely nature was lost to men during the Middle Ages; how comparatively untouched human life was by association with the countless aspects of sea and sky; how generally the union between men and the sublime house in which they lived was broken. For several centuries the great mass of men and women were so estranged from nature that they forgot their kinship. It is true that there were in every generation men and women to whom the beauty of the world did not appeal in vain, but it was a beauty obscured by mists of superstition, and the perception of which was painfully limited by lack of the deeper

insight and the larger vision.   Woods, flowers, and
streams, so close at hand, so intimately associated with
the richest experiences, could not wholly fail of that
charm which they possess to-day; but while these
lovely details were seen, the picture as a whole was
invisible.   The popular ballads and epics are not
lacking in pretty bits of description and sentiment, but
nature is wholly subordinate ; the sublime background
against which all modern life is set is invisible.

It is difficult to imagine a time when men had no
eye for the landscape, and yet it is one of the most
notable facts about Petrarch that he was the first man
of his period to show any interest in that great vision
which a lofty mountain opens, and which has for the
men of to-day a delight so poignant as to be almost
painful.   Dante had struck some deep notes which
showed clearly enough that he was alive to the mystery
and marvel of the physical world, but Petrarch was the
earliest of those who have seen clearly the range and
significance of nature as it stands related to the life of
men.   He celebrated the charms of Vaucluse in letters
which might have been written by Maurice de Guérin,
so modern is their tone, so contemporaneous their note
of intimate companionship.   "This lovely region," he
writes, "is as well adapted as possible to my studies
and labours, so long as iron necessity compels me to
live outside of Italy.   Morning and evening the hills
throw welcome shadows ; in the valleys are sun-warmed
gaps, while far and wide stretches a lovely landscape,
in which the tracks of animals are seen oftener than

those of men. Deep and undisturbed silence reigns
everywhere, only broken now and then by the murmur
of falling waters, the lowing of cattle, and the songs of
birds." But it was the ascent of Mont Ventoux,
accompanied by his younger brother and two country-
men, which stamps Petrarch as one of the great dis-
coverers of the natural world. There are few more
significant or fascinating moments in the history of human development than that which gave Petrarch his
first glimpse of the beautiful landscape about Avignon,
from the crest of the hill; it marked the beginning of a new era in the history of the human soul.
That the majesty of the outlook so overwhelmed
Petrarch that it drove him back upon himself, brought
all his sins to mind, and sent him to the "Confessions of St. Augustine," showed that he was still the
child of his age; but the longing which led him to
make the ascent, despite the warning of the old herdsmen at the foot of the mountain, showed that he was
also a man of the new time, and that he had unconsciously assumed the attitude of the modern mind
towards nature.

The redemption of nature from the shadow of sin
which, to the mediæval mind, rested upon and dark-
ened it, has been very slowly accomplished; but the
poets, the naturalists, and the scientists have taught us
much, and our hearts have taught us more. Nature
has become not only an inexhaustible delight, a constant and fascinating friend, but the most vital and
intimate of teachers; in fact, it is from the study of

nature, in one form or another, that much of the
advance in educational efficiency has come; not the
improvements in method, but the freshening and deepening of the educational aim and spirit. Nature,
through the discoveries of science, has restored balance to the mind, and sanity to the spirit of men by
correcting the false perspective of abstract thinking, by
flooding the deepest questions with new light, by bringing into activity a set of faculties almost disused, and
by adding immeasurably to the resources of the human
spirit.   In the Middle Ages attention was concentrated
upon the soul, and men learned much from their
eager and passionate self-questioning; but it was a
very inadequate and distorted view of life which they
reached, because one of the great sources of revelation
was left untouched.   In modern times the world of
nature has been searched with tireless patience, great
truths relating to man's place in the sublime movement of the universe have come to light, and the distorted vision of the inward world has been corrected
by the clear vision of the outward world.   The study
of nature has yielded a new conception of the nature
of the divine will expressed through law, of the divine
design interpreted by the order and progress of the
phenomena of the physical universe, of the marvellous
beauty of the divine mind which Tennyson was thinking of when, looking long and steadfastly into the
depths of a slow-moving stream, he cried out in awe
and wonder, "What an imagination God has!"

Men are saner, healthier, wiser, since they began to

find God in nature and to receive the facts of nature as a divine revelation. The soul has looked away from herself and out into the marvellous universe, and learned from a new teacher the wonder, the beauty, and the greatness of her life.

THE POWER WHICH LIBERATES.

In Dr. Parsons' fine lines "On a Bust of Dante" there is a verse which suggests even more than it conveys : —

> " Faithful if this wan image be,
>   No dream his life was — but a fight !
> Could any Beatrice see
>   A lover in that anchorite ?
> To that cold Ghibeline's gloomy sight
>   Who could have guessed the visions came
> Of Beauty, veiled with heavenly light,
>   In circles of eternal flame ? "

The contrast between the outward and the inward life — the one all shadow and hardship, the other all splendour and affluence — has never been more impressively disclosed than in the story of the Florentine poet whose brief and bitter years have in their train a fame of universal range and almost piercing lustre. It may be doubted whether the " Divine Comedy " would have been so widely treasured if the story of the singer had been less pathetic and significant. If its authorship were unknown, it would still remain one of the incomparable achievements of art ; but the personal anguish behind it lends it that spell which issues out of experience, and to which no human heart can be wholly indifferent. There are many to whom the poem would be incomprehensible; there are few to whom the poet would appeal in vain. If his thought often took wing beyond the range of the common thought, his experience shared with all humanity that visitation of sorrow from which none wholly escape. The very completeness of the shipwreck of his personal fortunes makes the greatness of his achievement the more impressive; and the hardness of his lot lends a new splendour to his imagination.

For Dante, the imagination meant not only the power of creating on a great scale, but also liberation from the iron bars of circumstance which imprisoned him. He was banished from Florence, but no decree could shut his thought out from the streets and squares that were so dear to him. It is true that he has spoken in memorable words of the sadness of revisiting in dreams alone the places one loves; but there was, nevertheless, in that power of passing at will from Verona to Florence, a resource of incalculable value. The body might be bound; the man was free. This faculty, which sets us free from so many of our limitations and gives us citizenship in all ages and countries, is not only the one creative power in us, but is also our greatest resource. No gift is so rare and none so priceless as a powerful and productive imagination. That it is rare, the mass of contemporary verse-writing demonstrates with almost pathetic conclusiveness; that it is above price, the great works of art abundantly

prove. But from the purely personal point of view —
the interest, the variety, and the power of the individual life — no gift is so much to be prized. To the
possessor of this magical faculty the outward happenings are, at the worst, of secondary importance.
Homer will not find blindness too great a trial, if Troy
still stands in his vision with the hosts contending
about it, and the white-armed Nausicaa still greets the
much-travelled Ulysses on the beach ; and Shakespeare could have borne heavier sorrows than most
men have known, the Forest of Arden, Prospero's
Island, and the enchanted woodland of the Midsummer
Night's Dream being open to him. Spenser could
find refuge from the tumult of Ireland in the dominion
of the Faery Queen ; Milton, with sealed eyes, solitary
in an age apostate to his faith and hope, saw Paradise
with undimmed vision ; and Browning, in the uproar,
contention, and uncertainty of this turbulent century,
heard Pippa, unconsciously touching the tragedy of
life at so many points, still serenely singing her song
of faith and peace.

It is doubtful whether any of us understand what
the imagination means to us simply as the liberating
force which throws the doors and windows open.
When imagination withers and art dies, discontent,
misery, and revolutions are in order. It is the outlook
through the windows, the breath of air through the
open door, that keeps men content in their workshops ;
where the outlook is shut off and the air no longer
comes fresh and vital into the close room the workers

grow reckless and hopeless. For without the imagination — the power to look through and beyond our conditions — life would be intolerable. Better a great activity of the imagination and hard conditions than ease of condition and poverty of imagination; for men are never so dangerous as when their bodies are fed and their souls starved. A perfectly comfortable society deprived of the resources of the imagination, would invite and foster the most desperate anarchism; for men live by ideas, not by things. A man who sees a great purpose shining before him can endure all hardness for the glory that is to come; the man who no longer has desires, because all his wants are met, suffers a swift deterioration of nature, and is at last the victim of his own prosperity. The Roman noble, in Mr. Arnold's striking poem, finds life unbearable because his passions are sated, his appetites fed, and his imagination dead. He is suffocated by his own luxury. Dante, on the other hand, feels keenly his condition, but lives more deeply and gloriously than any man of his time because, in spite of the hardness of his lot, his imagination travels through all worlds, and beyond the barren hour discerns the splendours of Paradise. The prophets, teachers, and poets, who alone have made life bearable, have been the children of the imagination, and have had the supreme consolation of looking through the limitations into which every man is born into the great heavens flaming with other worlds than ours. For it is the imagination which realises the soul in things material and reads this universe of matter as a symbol, and so liberates us from the oppression which comes from mere magnitude and mass ; which discerns the inner meaning of the family, the Church, and the State, and, in spite of all frailties and imperfections, makes their divine origin credible ; which discovers the end of labour in power, of self-denial in freedom, of hardness and suffering in the perfecting of the soul. " I am never confused," said Emerson, " if I see far enough ; " and the imagination is the faculty which sees. Of the several faculties by the exercise of which men live, it is most necessary, practical, and vital ; and yet so little is it understood that it is constantly spoken of as something very beautiful in its activity, but the especial property of artists, poets, and dreamers !

THE UNCONSCIOUS ARTIST.

GOETHE used to smile when he was asked for an explanation of certain oracular or enigmatical sayings in the second part of " Faust." One of the minor pleasures of his old age was the consciousness that a great many disciples believed in their hearts that he had the key to the mysteries in his keeping, and that, if he chose, he could answer all the questions which had tormented the race from the beginning. There was a mysterious reticence, an Olympian reserve, about the old poet which went far to confirm this faith, and it must be said that Goethe did not go out of his way to dispel the illusion. No man knew better than he the limitations of knowledge ; he was too great and too honest to play with his public ; but when the great man has become an absolute sovereign, and has grown gray upon the solitary throne, and when, moreover, he has the resource of humour for his waning days, he may be pardoned for suffering men to entertain a belief in an infallibility of the reality of which he is sometimes half persuaded himself. " Master," said an awestruck young man in Victor Hugo's *salon* one evening not long before the poet's death, " this age has known many great spirits, but thou art the greatest of them all." "Yes," answered the old poet, without even a ghost of a smile, "and the age is passing, and I, too, am nearing the end!" Goethe was free from the colossal egotism of Hugo, and, even if he had possessed it, his humour would have protected him from any expression of it; but Goethe was not above the pleasure of being thought great, nor could he deny himself the satisfaction of being regarded as an oracle. Probably no man could resist an appeal to self-love so unsolicited and so beguiling.

There is no reason to doubt, however, that Goethe sometimes took refuge in silence because he could not answer the questions that were propounded to him about his own work. When such questions were asked he always assumed an oracular manner which deepened the impression that, if he chose, he might disclose very deep things, and withdraw the veil from very great mysteries. This evasion must not be set down to his discredit, however; it was the refuge of a man who knew too much and had done too many great things to dread that confession of ignorance from which a man of lesser range and mind might have shrunk. He had a touch of vanity like his fellows, however, and his turn for proverbial and epigrammatic speech made the oracular tone very attractive to him. The fundamental fact about the matter is, however, that there were many things in Goethe's work of which he could not have given a clear explanation, because, like every other great mind, he builded better than he knew. The critical habit was strong with him, and very few men have thought more exhaustively and thoroughly about the principles and processes of art than he; nevertheless, it remains true that the deepest and richest parts of his work were the creation of the unconscious rather than the conscious Goethe.

It was one of Goethe's most profound and fruitful ideas that what a man would do greatly he must do with his whole nature. He was the first great artist to formulate clearly the fundamental law that the artist is conditioned by his own nature, that art rests upon life, and that there is, therefore, in a true work of art an expression of a man's complete nature, — his body, his mind, and his heart. For the artist is not a mechanic who skilfully devises processes to secure a certain definite end; he is not a trained mind and a trained hand working by rule and system; he is a spontaneous and original force in the world, as mysterious to himself as to others, — full of unknown possibilities; fed, sleeping and waking, by a thousand invisible streams of impulse and power; expanded unconsciously to himself by the very process of living; developed as much by feeling as by thought; and slowly gathering to himself a great inward wealth of knowledge, vitality, beauty, and power. When at last such a nature produces, it does not work mechanically; it creates by giving itself; by expressing what is deepest and truest in itself through the forms of art. In every product of mechanical skill, however perfect, the process can be discovered; but no analysis ever yet surprised nature in the making of a flower. The living thing that reaches its perfection ·by growth, being, so to speak, all of a piece, and attaining its development by the unfolding of itself, eludes the keenest analysis and remains a mystery in spite of the almost infinite patience of science. In like manner, a work of art, being a growth and not a mechanical product, remains mysterious and inexplicable even to its creator. There are certain elements in it which he consciously contributes; there are other elements which are there without his planning or knowledge. A work of art is the joint product of the conscious and the unconscious man, and there is, consequently, much in every such work which transcends, not the nature, but the mind, of the artist. For every great man builds better than he knows.

It is not difficult to believe, therefore, that there were things in " Faust " which Goethe could not completely explain. The poem was, in fact, of wider range than he knew. Its significance as an interpretation or representation of life was not undervalued by him, but there are many truths in it of which he did not perceive the full import, and later students find in it much which is unquestionably present in it, but of which Goethe was unconscious. The conscious Goethe, planning, brooding, shaping, did much; but the unconscious Goethe, living, feeling, suffering, acting, did more. And this is true not only of " Faust," but of the Book of Job, of the " Iliad," of the " Divine Comedy," and of " Lear " and " The Tempest." It is certainly not true that the great artist is the tool of an impulse, an irresponsible inspiration, and puts forth the sublimest conceptions without any idea of their depth and range. Those who believe that the author of " Hamlet " and " The Tempest " had a magical gift of dramatic expression, but no comprehension of philosophic relations and values, cannot have read " Troilus and Cressida " with any care. Shakespeare knew what he was doing when he wrote " Lear," as did Goethe when he wrote " Faust," and Tennyson when he wrote " In Memoriam ;" in each case, however, there was inwrought into the very nature of the poet a prophetic element which gave his thought a range beyond that of his experience, and his vision a clearness and scope beyond those of his thought. It is the peculiar gift of the man of genius that when he portrays the individual he brings the type before us, when he gives the fact he suggests the truth which interprets it, when he reports the phenomena he reveals the law behind it ; and so he constantly, and for the most part, unconsciously, lets us into the universal by setting before us the particular.

THE LAW OF OBEDIENCE.

In reading Marlowe one is brought face to face, not only with tragic situations, but with the elemental tragedy, — the tragedy which has its rise in the conflict between the infinite desires of the soul and rigid restrictions of its activity. The master of " the mighty line " never learned that lesson of self-mastery which Shakespeare studied so faithfully; he was always wasting his immense force on the impossible, and matching his powerful genius against those immutable conditions imposed upon men, not to dwarf but to develop them. In art no less than in morals supreme achievement is conditioned not only upon a free use of one's powers, but upon a clear recognition of their limits; the great artist never attempts the impossible. In " Tamburlaine " Marlowe strove not only to portray a personality striving to transcend human limitations, but to pass beyond them himself by the sheer force of his genius; but neither the conqueror nor the dramatist evaded the play of that law which binds ultimate freedom to immediate obedience. Shakespeare, on the other hand, achieved the most impressive success in modern literature when he dealt with the same problem in " Lear," — a success based on a clear perception of the exact limits within which the human personality may express itself.

We touch at this point not only the essence of the deepest tragedy, but the secret of the highest art ; for the elemental tragedy is the struggle between the will and the conditions imposed upon its expression, and the secret of art resides, not only in the depth and vitality of the artist's mastery of his materials, but also in the clearness of his perception of the decisive line between the possible and the impossible. The Classical writers, with their delicate sense of proportion, harmony, and form, never attempted to pass beyond the limits of a sound art ; they were sometimes formal and cold, but they were never tumultuous, unbalanced, and lawless. In Sophocles, for instance, one never loses consciousness of the presence of a genius which, dealing with the most perplexing and terrible questions of destiny, is never tempted to pass the bounds of clear and definite artistic expression, but sustains the theme to the end with a masterful self-restraint and majesty of repose. In that noble balance, based on the harmony, not on the subjection of the heart and mind of the artist, one gets a glimpse of one of the great ends of art ; which is not to express but to suggest that which transcends human thought and speech. For the great play, statue, picture, speech are prophetic, and find their fulfilment, not in themselves, but in the imagination which comes under their spell ; the more complete their beauty, therefore, the more powerfully do they affirm the existence of a beauty beyond themselves. The definiteness of Greek art was not a limitation ; it was a source of transcendent power. It is true, it shut the Greek artist out of some great fields; but he was not ready to enter them, and the divine apparition of beauty always moved with his work and issued out of it as a soul is revealed by a body as beautiful as itself. The Venus of Milos is not the image of a saint, but there is that in the mutilated statue which makes the divine perfection not only credible but actual.

For there is, in supreme excellence of any kind, an immense exhilaration for the human spirit, — a power of impulsion, which leads or drives it out of itself into new spiritual quests and ventures. Dante had no thought of a re-awakening of the mind of man; he did not discern that thrilling chapter of history so soon to be written; but to that great movement the " Divine Comedy " was one of the chief contributing forces. The production of such a masterpiece was in itself a new liberation of the human spirit, and set the currents of imagination and action flowing freely once more. It matters little whether a great book has definite teaching for men or not; it is always a mighty force for liberation. Greek art had its limitations of theme and manner, but its perfection brought constantly before the mind that ultimate perfection, which it evaded so far as definite treatment was concerned, but the existence of which was implied in its own existence, and the fuller revelation of which it was always unconsciously predicting.

This thought hints at the working out in art of that deepest and most mysterious of all the laws of life, which declares that he who would save his life must lose it : that sublime contradiction which seems always to be assailing man's happiness and is always preserving it. The restraint of the great Classical dramatists, which to a man like Marlowe seems a surrender of power, is, in reality, the disclosure of a power so great that it makes one forget the limitations of the artist by giving us the freedom of the art. For when a man submits himself to the laws of his craft he ceases to be its bondman and becomes its master. Marlowe evaded or refused this submission, and his work, while it discloses great force, makes us painfully aware of limitations and crudity; Shakespeare, on the other hand, cheerfully submitted to the laws of his craft, and his work, by reason of its balance and harmony, con-veys a sense of limitless power, of boundless capacity for mastering the most difficult problems of life and art. Never was the glorious commonplace that a man becomes free by obedience more beautifully illustrated.

The Greek artist registered one of the most decisive advances in human thought when for the Oriental indeterminateness he substituted his own definiteness; and the human spirit took a great forward step when it discerned that by subjection to the law of its growth it would ultimately achieve that freedom which the Oriental mind had attempted to grasp at once, and which it had failed to seize. Between Plato and Aristotle and the Oriental thinkers before them there was a great gulf fixed which remains to-day impassable, although many fragile and fantastic structures have of late years swung airily over the abyss. In the Greek thought the foundations of Western civilisation are set, and in that thought rest also the eternal foundations of art. For personality, freedom, and responsibility were the fundamental Greek ideas, and they are the ideas which underlie Western life and art. The Greek artist recognised the integrity of his own nature, and discerned his consequent freedom and responsibility. He did not lose himself in God, nor merge himself in nature ; he stood erect ; he worshipped, he observed, and he created. He did not, through failure of clear thought, attempt the impossible, as did his fellow in the farther East ; he saw clearly the limitations of his faculty, and he discerned that freedom and power lay in accepting, not in ignoring, those limitations. He constructed the Parthenon instead of miles of rock-hewn temple ; and for monsters, and gigantic, unreal symbols he carved the Olympian Zeus and the inimitable Venus of the Louvre Gallery. He peopled the world with divinities, and in his marvellous illustration of the fecundity of the human spirit, and of its power, he created an art which not only affirms the integrity of the soul, but predicts its immortality. There have been great artists from that day to this, and art has passed through many phases, but the old law finds constant illustration ; and between Tennyson and Swinburne, as between Shakespeare and Marlowe, one discerns the gain and the waste of power inherent, the first in self-restraint, the second in self-assertion.

STRUGGLE IN ART.

MARLOWE'S excess and lack of restraint debarred him from the highest achievement as an artist; but his vitality and force were qualities of lasting attraction and incalculable value. By virtue of his rich and passionate nature he stands in close proximity to the great group from whose magic circle he was shut out only by his failure to obey the laws of his art. Few writers have possessed a force of imagination and passion so great and so impressive; and it is interesting to note how much more quickly men are drawn to the Titan than to the Olympian; for struggle is pathetically universal, and the repose of harmonious achievement pathetically rare among men. The greater the art, the slower the recognition, as a rule. The impression made by a lawless or unregulated force is always more immediate than that made by a mastered and harmonised power. The rending of a cliff makes every observer conscious of the force of the explosive, but how few ever think of the force put forth in lifting an oak from its rootage in the earth to the great height where all the winds of heaven play upon it !

The "storm and stress" period moves all hearts and stirs in the young imagination one knows not what dreams and desires, but when the ferment of spirit is past, and the new thought has taken its enduring form, what a sense of disappointment comes to a host of aspiring souls ! The struggle touched and intoxicated them with a sense of something not only great but akin to their own experience; the clarification and final expression of the new spirit in art seems somehow remote and cold. When the "Sorrows of Werther" appeared a thrill ran through Germany; but when "Tasso" and "Iphigenia" were given to the world with what indifference they were received! The boy reads "The Robbers" with bated breath, but ten years later he knows that the Schiller of the Wallenstein trilogy was an incomparably greater writer than the Schiller of "The Robbers." Revolt is easier than reconstruction; at the barricade every one is swept by a consuming enthusiasm, but the moment the attempt is made to give the new time order and stability, divisions and indifference appear. Struggle, however noble, is for the moment; achievement has something of eternity in it. The Titan is always a striking figure, but it is the Olympian who endures and rules.

The element of struggle is, however, a part of the greatest art, and the motive of much of the highest work done by men has been the harmonising of antagonistic forces and the final and beautiful synthesis of contending ideas. It is by struggle that life is broadened, and the human spirit freed from many of its limitations; and there is nothing nobler in man than that constant dissatisfaction with his condition which provokes the struggle. The race is always reaching forward to grasp better things than it yet possesses. It is haunted by visions of perfection, and driven on by aspirations and dreams which will not suffer it to rest in any present achievement. This discontent is not a superficial restlessness; it is the evidence of the infinite possibilities of man's nature, and of his inability to stop short of complete development. All literature bears witness to this arduous, sorrowful, inspiring struggle for a more harmonious life, so often defeated, so constantly renewed.

In the record of this sublime drama, of which man himself is the protagonist, there is found one great means of escape from those limitations of experience which give us such constant pain and fill us with a consuming desire to escape from ourselves. " Sensations of all kinds have been crowding upon me," writes Amiel, — " the delights of a walk under the rising sun, the charms of a wonderful view, longing for travel, and thirst for joy, hunger for work, for emotion, for life, dreams of happiness and of love. A passionate wish to live, to feel, to express, stirred the depths of my heart. It was a sudden reawakening of youth, a flash of poetry, a renewing of the soul, a fresh growth of the wings of desire. I was overpowered by a host of conquering, vagabond, adventurous aspirations. I forgot my age, my obligations, my duties, my vexations, and youth leapt within me as though life were beginning again. It was as though something explosive had caught fire, and one's soul were scattered to the four winds ; in such a mood one would fain devour the whole world, experience everything, see everything. Faust's ambition enters into one — universal desire — a horror of one's own prison cell. One throws off one's hair shirt, and one would fain gather the whole of nature into one's arms and heart."

How often Amiel made the rounds of his cell, and how vainly he strove to break the bars of his temperament, the world knows from that incomparable record, in the writing of which his spirit found the escape sought for in vain in other directions. Self-contained, reticent, shy, how few dreamed of the turbulence in the soul of the formal and didactic teacher in the formal and rather pedantic little city of Calvin and Rousseau ! Without the " Journal," the struggle and the wealth of Amiel's nature would never have been known ; it adds another chapter to that book of life in which the race records its secret hopes and despairs. And is it not pathetically significant that the motive with which the Greek dramatists dealt with so strong a hand reappears in this quiet drama enacted in the soul of the Genevan Professor of Moral Philosophy ? On the widest as on the narrowest stage it is the motive which all men understand, because it is a part of every human experience. The Old Testament, the Epics of Homer, the " Divine Comedy," the plays of Shakespeare, and " Faust " are among its greatest records, but its story is in all lives.

To every man comes the struggle, to a few great writers the power to interpret the struggle and predict or portray its issue in immediate reconciliation or in ultimate achievement. And so art becomes an avenue of escape from the prison of personal experience, not only by taking us out of ourselves, but by disclosing the identity of our individual struggle with the universal struggle of humanity. It opens the door out of the particular into the universal, and it constantly predicts the final resolution of discords into harmony, the ultimate reconciliation of contending ideas and forces; and when, as in " Lear," it gives no suggestion of an answer to the problems involved, the very magnitude of the drama which it unfolds compels the inference of an adequate solution on some other and larger stage.

THE PASSION FOR PERFECTION.

It is one of the pains of the artistic temperament that its exaltations of mood and its ecstasies of spirit must be largely solitary. The air of this century is not genial to that intimacy with beauty which solicits easy interchange of confidences among those who enjoy it. The mass of men are preoccupied and unsensitive on that side of life which has for the artist the deepest reality; they are given over to pursuits which are imperative in their demands, and fruitful in their rewards, but which lead far from the pursuit of beauty. There have been times when the artistic temper, if not widely shared, was generally understood, and such times will come again when the modern world becomes more thoroughly harmonised with itself; meantime the man who has the joys of the artistic temperament will accept them as a sufficient consolation for its pains.

For the essence of this temperament is not so much its sensitiveness to every revelation of the beautiful as its passion for perfection. There is in the life of the artist an element of pain, which never goes beyond a dumb sense of discontent in men of coarser mould; for the artist is compelled to live with his ideals !

Other men have occasional glimpses of their ideals; the artist lives his life in their presence and under their searching glances. A man is in the way to become genuine and noble when his ideals draw near and make their home with him instead of floating before him like summer clouds, forever dissolving and reforming on the distant horizon; but he is also in the way of very real anguish of spirit. Our ideals, when we establish them under our own roofs, are as relentless as the Furies who thronged about Orestes; they will not let us rest. The world may applaud, but if they avert their faces reputation is a mockery and success a degradation. The passion for perfection is the divinest possession of the soul, but it makes all lower gratifications, all compromises with the highest standards, impossible. The man whom it dominates can never taste the easy satisfactions which assuage the thirst of those who have it not; for him it must always be the best or nothing.

Flaubert, Mr. James tells us, ought always to be cited as one of the martyrs of the plastic idea; the "torment of style" was never eased in his case, and despite his immense absorption and his tireless toil, he failed to touch the invisible goal for which he set out. "Possessed," says one of his critics, who was also a devotee of the supreme excellence, "of an absolute belief that there exists but one way of expressing one thing, one word to call it by, one adjective to qualify, one verb to animate it, he gave himself to superhuman labour for the discovery, in every phrase, of that word, that verb, that epithet. In this way he believed in some mysterious harmony of expression, and when a true word seemed to him to lack euphony, still went on seeking another with invincible patience, certain that he had not yet got hold of the unique word. . . . A thousand preoccupations would beset him at the same moment, always with this desperate certitude fixed in his spirit, — among all the expressions in the world, there is but *one* — one form, one mode — to express what I want to say."

To a mind capable of absolute devotion, such an ideal as Flaubert set before him not only draws him on through laborious days, deaf to the voices of pleasure, but consumes him with an inward fire. The aim of the novelist was not simply to set the best words in the best order; it was to lay hold upon perfection; to touch those ultimate limits beyond which the human spirit cannot go, and where that spirit stands face to face with the absolute perfection. This passionate pursuit of the finalities of form and expression is as far removed from the pursuit of mere craftsmanship as art itself is separated from mere mechanical skill; and yet so little is the real significance of art understood among us that it is continually confused with craftsmanship, and spoken of as something apart from a man's self, something born of skill and akin to the mechanical, instead of being the very last and supreme outflowing of that within us which is spontaneous and inspired. In a fine burst of indignation at this profanation of one of the greatest words in human speech, Mr. Aldrich says : —

" ' Let art be all in all,' one time I said,
    And straightway stirred the hypercritic gall ;
    I said not, ' Let technique be all in all,'
But art — a wider meaning.   Worthless, dead —
The shell without its pearl, the corpse of things,
Mere words are, till the spirit lends them wings ;
The poet who breathes no soul into his lute
Falls short of art : 't were better he were mute.

" The workmanship wherewith the gold is wrought
    Adds yet a richness to the richest gold :
    Who lacks the art to shape his thought, I hold,
Were little poorer if he lacked the thought.
The statue's slumbers were unbroken still
Within the marble, had the hand no skill.
Disparage not the magic touch that gives
The formless thought the grace whereby it lives ! "

Flaubert did not touch the goal, in spite of his heroic toil, and largely because of that toil. For he sought too strenuously, with intention too insistent and dominant ; he was driven by his passion instead of being inspired by it. It is as true of our relations with our ideals as of our relations with our friends that we must preserve our independence ; our ideals must lead, but they must not tyrannise over us. There is something in us which even our ideals must respect, and that something is our own individuality. The perfection which a man pursues must be the perfection of his own quality, not a perfection which is foreign to him. It is himself which he is to raise to the highest point of power, not something outside of himself. Flaubert understood this, for he once wrote : " In literature the best chance one has is by following one's temperament and exaggerating it." Nevertheless, one of the defects of his work is the fact that its perfection is not the perfection of his temperament, — is, indeed, a kind of objective perfection, which seems at times detached so entirely from temperament that it is hard and cold and devoid of atmosphere. To this detachment is due perhaps the failure to secure that ultimate excellence of which his whole life was one arduous pursuit. For Flaubert rarely passed beyond the stage of effort ; his pen rarely caught that native rhythm which we detect in Scott and Thackeray and Tolstoi at their best, — that perfect adequacy, manifested in perfect ease, which makes us forget the toil in the perfection of the work, and which assures us that the slow hand of the artisan has become the swift hand of the artist. Surely the way of perfection is straight and narrow, and few there be who follow it to the end !

CRITICISM AS AN INTERPRETER.

A GOOD deal has been said about the influence of criticism as a restraining and corrective force constantly and effectively brought to bear on writers; and it is probably true that no small gains in the direction of better and sounder work have been made as a result of criticism, even when it has been inadequate and coarse in tone. There is good reason to believe that Tennyson felt keenly the unnecessary offensiveness with which the tinge of sentimentality and the defective energy of expression in his work given to the world in 1832 were pointed out by more than one critical writer of the time; nevertheless, the young poet profited by correction so ungraciously administered, and what might have developed into an unsound strain became, ten years later, the evidence of a peculiar ripeness and beauty. In many cases, doubtless, criticism, even when it has fallen below its highest levels, has been a useful teacher and monitor, and in this way has rendered genuine service to literature. But this service of criticism is, after all, secondary and incidental; for it is the writer, and not the critic, who makes literature, not only in the sense of creating, but also of determining its forms. The critic often tells

the writer facts about himself which are of lasting
value in his artistic education, but in the end it is
the writer who marks out the lines along which the
critic must move.

Criticism was long oblivious of this fundamental fact
in its relation to distinctively creative work ; it was long
under the impression that the final authority resided in
itself rather than in the work upon which it passed
judgment with entire confidence in its own competency. It was not until criticism passed into the
hands of men of insight and creative power that it
discovered its chief function to be that of comprehension, and its principal service that of interpretation.
Not that it has surrendered its function of judging
according to the highest standards, but that it has
discovered that the forms of excellence change from
time to time, and that the question with regard to a work
of art is not whether it conforms to types of excellence
already familiar, but whether it is an ultimate expression of beauty or power. In every case the artist
creates the type, and the critic proves his competency
by recognising it ; so that while the critic holds the
artist to rigid standards of veracity and craftsmanship, it
is the artist who lays down the law to the critic. As
an applied art, based on deduction, and constructing
its canons apart from the material which literature
furnishes, criticism was notable mainly for its fallibility.
As an art based on induction, and framing its laws according to the methods and principles illustrated in
the best literature, it has advanced from a secondary

to a leading place among the literary forms now most widely employed and most widely influential.

The real service of criticism is to the reader rather than to the writer, and it serves literature chiefly by making its recognition on the part of the reader more prompt and more complete. A work of art does not need to be preserved, it preserves itself; there is in it a vitality which endures indifference and survives neglect. What is often lost, however, is the immediate influence of such a work. It has happened again and again in the history of literature that a great book has been long unrecognised; and a resource which might have enriched life has been put aside until men were educated to receive and use it. It is as an educative force that criticism has developed its most immediate and, perhaps, its most lasting usefulness.

For while great works of art do not need the aid of criticism to preserve them from the danger of actual disappearance, they do need its service as an interpreter. What Addison had to say about Milton did not protect the Puritan poet from any danger of permanent obscurity, but it went far toward making a clearer understanding of his greatness possible. It was a service to the English people, and, in so much as it opened their eyes to an excellence which had been widely denied, it was also a service to English literature. The old dramas which Lamb loved with such missionary zeal were in no sense dependent upon that zeal for their preservation; but they gained by it a recognition more general and more intelligent than they

had won even from the generation which had heard
their noble or terrible lines declaimed on the stage.
Cromwell would have remained the great soul he was had
Carlyle passed him by, but it was Carlyle's searching
insight and victorious art which restored the Protector
to his place in the history and the heart of England.
To comprehend a work of art, a certain degree of
education must be attained ; and the greater and more
original the work of art, the deeper and more thorough
the education required.   For it is the peculiar quality
of genius to be prophetic, and to create in advance —
sometimes far in advance — of general comprehension.
Society must grow into the larger thought which at first
often escapes it, and grow into the openmindedness to
which beauty in a new form successfully makes its appeal.   The greater writers, whose creative energy finds
new channels and manifests itself under unfamiliar
aspects, are always in advance of the general capacity
of appreciation, and are always in need of interpreters ;
and this office of interpretation has become the chief
function of criticism.   Taine interprets English literature by effectively, if somewhat coarsely, filling in the
background of the environment and experience of the
race ; while Sainte-Beuve interprets the book by sug-
gesting with delicate but impressive skill the personality of the writer.

When a man like Goethe takes up criticism, its
range and power become at once apparent.   Insight
is substituted for literary tradition, and sympathy is
emphasised as the keyword of the critical art.   We are

no longer dealing with a police magistrate intent upon the rigid administration of a petty local code, but with a man of universal interests, familiar with all standards, quick to feel all kinds of excellence, and eager to discern in a work of art, not only its relation to the past, but its fresh revelation of what is in man and in his life, and its new disclosure of the exhaustless power of the imagination to create forms. After such a critic has spoken, and has suggested the possibilities of criticism, it is not surprising to find so many minds of the highest order drawn to it. So far from being the secondary or derivative art which it is often declared to be, criticism, on its higher plane, involves the possession of an insight, a breadth of intelligence, and a faculty of expression which in their combination must be regarded as belonging to the sphere of the creative forces. Coleridge, Carlyle, Sainte-Beuve, Amiel, Arnold, Emerson, and Lowell represent criticism at its best, and are, therefore, the men by whose work it must be judged.

THE EDUCATIONAL QUALITY OF CRITICISM.

THE prime characteristic of the work of the great critics is interpretation, and its deepest influence is educational. It is true that all art is educational, and that literature, as Matthew Arnold long ago said in one of his suggestive school reports, contains the best possible material for education; but criticism is peculiarly and definitely educational, because it brings into clear light the significance of literature as a whole. The immediate and vital relationship between art and life, which has given literature an entirely new meaning to modern men, was largely discerned and disclosed by the great modern critics. To them we owe not only clear ideas of the specific work and personal quality of each writer, but clear ideas of his relation to his time and to his race, — of his significance in the development of literature and in the history of the human soul. There is a distinct and definite educational value in the comprehension of Montaigne's relation to his age, of the influences which found their expression in Voltaire and Rousseau, and of the facts of race inheritance and social condition which made so deep an impress on the artistic temperament of Tourguenieff. There is indeed no educational

material of such interest and importance as that preserved in books, because nowhere else has the life of
men made a record at once so frank, so searching,
and so appealing. It was a profound thought of
Froebel's that the true teacher of each individual is
the race, and that what the race has thought, felt, and
accomplished is the richest material for educational
uses. And literature, being the fullest and frankest
revelation of what is in men and of what they have
experienced, is the most vital and persuasive teacher
of humanity.

It is and has been the function of criticism in the
hands of the masters of the art to bring into clear light
this educational significance of literature ; to trace its
intimate and necessary relations with the time which
produced it ; to indicate the racial elements which enter
into it ; to point out the impress of personality ; and
to set each great work in true relation to that disclosure
of the nature of man of which art has kept so faithful a
record. In thus dealing with literary works as parts of
one great expression of the soul, criticism has not lost
its judicial spirit nor parted with its instinct for perfection of form. It has simply struck a true balance
between the human and the artistic elements in works
of literature ; it has shown the rootage of art in life ; it
has set the man beside his work, and made the work
the revelation of the man. The value of the general
service of such a new reading of literature cannot be
estimated, — so wide, so deep, and so subtle are those
educational influences which play upon the spirits of

men as part of the atmosphere which they breathe.
This is, however, a service to literature itself which is
often overlooked. The quality of disinterestedness,
upon which Mr. Arnold insisted at the very beginning
of his career as a critic, carries with it an inevitable
enlargement of thought. It is impossible to study
literary works as they appear fresh from widely differ-
ing conditions of race and individual life without
receiving, consciously or unconsciously, an education
of a very high order. Insular ignorance, class prejudice, national antagonism, race hostility, individual
prepossession and limitation are insensibly modified by
contact with life, unifying such a variety of conditions,
and revealing itself with equal authority through such
different forms of expression. The men are few whose
literary creeds can remain provincial in the face of the
catholicity of modern criticism. One may be wedded
to Romanticism, but he must be uncommonly unre-
sponsive if he fails to feel the power of such verse as
Landor and Arnold have given us. In these days it
is possible to be a lover of Flaubert and De Maupassant and yet enjoy George Sand; to care for
Corneille and yet recognise the power of Ibsen.

To put aside accidental methods, accepted standards, and personal prepossessions, and with open
mind to search each work of literature for its aim, its
reality, and its excellence, is not only to receive that
kind of education which affects the quality of a man's
nature, but to make it easier for the writer with the
new word and the new spirit to secure a hearing. Many

changes have taken place since Rabelais found it necessary to veil his attack on the educational methods of
the Church ; a man may now speak his thought without
peril to his head. But freedom of opinion was more
easily won than freedom of artistic expression. Even
in our own time there has been more than one demon-
stration of the danger which the artist faces when he
ventures into a fresh field and employs a new method.
Carlyle, Browning, Ibsen, and Whitman remind us, in
different chapters of their experience, that artistic toler-
ance has not yet come to perfect flower, and that
disinterestedness is not yet universal. Nevertheless, it
remains true that the conception of literature was
never so broad as at this moment, and there have
never been so many intelligent persons eager to recognise beauty, truth, and power, however strangely garbed.
When a critic so fastidious as Matthew Arnold recognises the literary quality shared in common by men as
diverse in temperament, idea, aim, and artistic method
as Wordsworth, Byron, Gray, Shelley, Heine, and
Tolstoï, the genuine catholicity of modern criticism
may be regarded as nearly complete. If the new
method must still win its way against prejudice and
conventional notions of art, it is rather because of indifference and inertia than of intentional antagonism.
In these days genius is in greater peril from premature
than from postponed recognition ; it is more likely to
be forced than to be repressed.

The larger thought of literature, as an expression of
the soul under the conditions of life and in the forms

of art, not only gives it a foremost place among the forces which civilise men, but gives it the stimulus of a great function and the freedom of a governing power. Criticism has not only opened the minds of readers, but it has invited writers to a freedom which they formerly were compelled to fight for; and who can doubt that in the long run this broader education of those to whom literature makes its appeal will react upon literary artists through provocation of earlier recognition, quicker response, and truer comprehension?

PLATO'S DIALOGUES AS LITERATURE.

WHEN Dr. Jowett's translation of Plato's "Dialogues" appeared in this country twenty years ago, a story was current that a Western newspaper closed its review of the work with the remark that Plato was one of the greatest of English prose writers! No finer tribute was ever paid to a translator, and that Plato got the credit of Dr. Jowett's beautiful skill was the most unaffected of compliments to the art of the accomplished Master of Balliol College. Plato had long been studied as a thinker, but the "Dialogues" as literature had received small attention. An occasional scholar had paused by the way in his philosophical studies to note the range and beauty of Plato's style, and to feel the charm of a literary quality rare at all times, and in no other instance possessed in equal degree by a thinker of the first order. For while there have been philosophical writers of force and clearness, Plato is the only great literary artist who has drawn upon all the resources of language to give philosophic thought vividness, adequacy, and perfection of expression.

The Greek genius gave many illustrations of the power of art to receive and communicate the most virile and powerful as well as the most subtle and delicate impress of the soul of man on his fellows and his time, but in nothing was the depth and force of the artistic impulse more impressively shown than in the ease of manner, the amplitude of mood, the ripeness of spirit, and perfection of form with which a system of thought was set forth. Under the spell of an artistic impulse so pervasive and so genuine, statesmanship became a matter of harmony and co-ordination quite as distinctly as sculpture or architecture, — for Pericles was as great an artist as Phidias ; oratory touched the sources of power in speech with an instinct as sure and true as that of the poet, — for Demosthenes was as genuine an artist as Sophocles. It was reserved for Plato, however, to discuss the profoundest questions of life, not with the aridity of a purely logical method, but with the freshness, the charm, and the grace of one to whom the divine Maker never ceased to be the divine Artist. The structure of the Parthenon discloses complete mastery of the art of building, but in the thought of its builders the pure construction of that noble treasure-house was never separated from the obvious and matchless beauty which makes it a thing of joy even in its ruins. In like manner, the most poetic of Greek thinkers did not divorce, even in thought, the massive structure of the universe from that beauty which clothes it in the sense in which beauty clothes the flower, by growing out of its hidden substance.

It is fortunate for the English-speaking peoples that this artist in thought and speech found a translator whose scholarship was equal to the large demands of the " Dialogues," and whose literary instinct and faculty were at once so responsive and so adequate. Plato could not have been translated save by a man of rare literary gift, and the possession of such a gift was the foremost qualification of Dr. Jowett. It is the fashion among some academicians to sneer at the literary faculty, but the fashion is a harmless one ; or, if it harms any one, harms only its votaries. The artistic element is the creative element, and is, therefore, distinctly the most precious quality of the human mind, — the quality which manifests itself in clear supremacy whenever character, thought, action, or achievement of any kind approaches perfection. Scholarship is comparatively common in the dullest age, but the artistic gift is rare in the greatest age. In Plato this element is so pervasive and so characteristic that to translate the " Dialogues " without reproducing their atmosphere would be like giving us the measurements of the Sistine Madonna without giving us contour, colour, or expression. The criticism which has sometimes assailed Dr. Jowett's translation because of its grace and fluency has been an unintentional tribute to the excellence of a work which, with refreshing disregard of academic notions, is not only accurate, but has dared to be as charming as its original !

In Dr. Jowett's full and ripe English, Plato's thought and expression are so faithfully preserved that one stands in no need of the Introductions to discern the quality which makes the " Dialogues " literature quite

as distinctly as they are philosophy. For the abiding
and varied charm of these discussions is the personality which pervades them. Plato was not a professional thinker, intent upon uncovering the logical order
of material and spiritual construction ; he was a richly
endowed personality, to whose mobile imagination and
quick artistic perceptions the movement of the world
was full of vitality, colour, and harmony. Thought was
never divorced from feeling, abstracted from the whole
of things ; it was involved in the general order and
inseparable from it. To comprehend the universe, one
must not only perceive its structure, but feel its fathomless beauty and bathe in its flowing tides of vitality.
This steadfast determination to see things in their vital movement gives us that harmony which is so pro-
nounced in Plato's thought, and gives us also those
charming groups which are associated with the " Dialogues." It was a consummate art which made each
discussion a chapter out of contemporary life, hinting
at the limitations of thought by skilfully bringing out
the limitations of the individual mind and experience,
and keeping always in view the dependence of thought
on temperament, education, and character ; to say
nothing of the luminous side-lights thrown on the profoundest themes by interlocutors who contribute not
only their thoughts, but themselves, to the debate, and
who give the hour and the question a rich and lasting
human interest. It is the constant spell of this human
interest which makes some of the dialogues — the
" Phædo," the " Phædrus," and the " Symposium," for

instance — literary classics. For the essence of art is that it is concrete instead of being abstract, and that it realises its thought in symbols and persons instead of putting it into propositions or maxims. If Plato had been simply a philosopher, he would have given the world the dissertation with which it has been familiar from the time of Aristotle to that of Kant ; but because he was also an artist he immersed his thought in the warm atmosphere of human life, and at every stage gave it the dramatic interest of intimate human association.

Those changing groups whose talk we seem to over-hear in so many pages of the " Dialogues " bring before us the mobility of the Ionic spirit, — that sensi-tiveness to form and colour, that quick interest in every-thing which touched the life of men, that instinct for the harmonious, which, in their combination, explain not only the Attic genius but the charm of Plato as a writer. There is an intense vitality in him, as there was in the Greek culture ; but it is restrained and harmonised. There is everywhere a strong sense of reality ; but it is reality in its very highest and most lasting forms. We are introduced to many persons, but most of them are of surpassing interest. The human element, in delicately drawn contrasts of char-acter, constantly divides attention with the thought, and while we climb the loftiest heights we are con-scious at every step of human companionship. The freshness, buoyancy, and vivacity of youth relieve the tension of speculation, and sometimes, as in the famous passage in the " Symposium," the strain of pure thought becomes a kind of introduction to a bit of drama of surpassing charm. Plato's imagination is revealed in the structure of the " Dialogues," and in his conception of the form in which his thought is cast ; it finds, however, specific disclosure in those fables which often contain the profoundest essence of his thought, but which are singularly beautiful in imagery and symbolism. It is found also in his style, in its variety, flexibility, fluidity, colour, and freshness, — a style delicate enough to receive the lightest impression, and stable enough to contain and communicate the profoundest thought. Says Mr. Pater: " No one, perhaps, has with equal power literally sounded the unseen depths of thought, and, with what may be truly called ' substantial ' word and phrase, given locality there to the mere adumbration, the dim hints and surmises, of the speculative mind."

Whoever opens the " Dialogues " knows that here there is the magic of art in lasting alliance with high and exacting thought, and that between these pages there is found not only the mind but the immortal life and freshness of Greece : " We shall meet a number of our youth there : we shall have a dialogue : there will be a torchlight procession in honour of the goddess, an equestrian procession, — a novel feature ! What? torches in their hands, passed on as they race? Ay, and an illumination through the entire night. It will be worth seeing ! "

THE POWER OF THE NOVEL.

THE interest excited by books of such substance and quality as Mrs. Ward's " Marcella " shows very clearly that the attractive power of fiction, after all these years of immense productivity in that department, is still unspent. Mr. Crawford, who is one of the most widely read novelists of the day, is of the opinion that the novel has passed its prime ; but neither the quality of work in fiction nor the popular interest in it shows as yet any evidence of decrepitude. On the contrary, at the close of a century which has been dominated by the novel as a literary form, fiction still remains, on the whole, the most real and vital of all the forms of expression which literary men are using, and is probably the form which exerts the widest influence upon the reading public. It would be unwise to predict the form of literature for which the men and women of the close of the twentieth century will care most, but the prediction that a hundred years from now the novel will still be universally read would be perhaps less rash than most literary predictions. In this country it cannot be said that we have produced any novelist of the first rank since Hawthorne, but we have produced a goodly number of novelists of high rank and a multi-

tude of short-story writers whose work betrays the presence of both nature and art in very uncommon and
delightful combination. The fact that we have produced no great novelist, and that the novel is still so
widely read, shows that its spell resides in some element aside from the individual power of the writer, and
that there is in the novel, as a form of literature, a
charm which the men and women of these days feel
very deeply.

That charm resides in the force, the directness, and
the delicacy with which fiction has interpreted and por-
trayed human life. The human drama in these later
days is engrossing to all serious-minded people, and
wherever the moral or spiritual fact or experience is
dramatized by the novelist with even a fair degree of
power, the novel which results is certain to have a
wide reading. The world-wide movement which has
already made such modifications in the social conditions, and which is silently effecting such a revolution
in the relations of men with men and of class with class,
finds its way into art through the insight, the observation, and the skill of the great novelist; and such a
book as " Marcella," entirely aside from its dramatic
effectiveness, gains an immense power simply from the
fact that it deals with questions in which everybody is
interested, and introduces with great directness that
human element which is to-day part and parcel of
every religious, political, or industrial problem. The
same impulse which gives the novel such a hold upon
readers produces also the great novelist; for behind

every widespread literary movement there is always a
vital movement of experience; and the great writer,
while his power resides in his own personality, is, in a
deep and true sense, the child of his time and the
interpreter of its thought.

This deeper source of interest must not tempt us to
forget, however, that the art of literature still involves
both pleasure and recreation, and that the sole end of
the book is not to instruct, inspire, and expand. These
are, indeed, the inevitable results of the greatest works
of art, but there is still a legitimate field for the solace,
the entertainment, and the recreation of mankind in
the hands of the story-tellers. It is safe to say, in the
face of all the tendency novels and the novels of purpose which have flooded the world in recent years —
and some of them are notable and permanent contri-
butions to literature — that men and women still crave
the novel of adventure and the romantic story. The
old story-tellers who recited the "Arabian Nights"
hundreds of years ago, and are still repeating them in
the East to-day, meet what is commonly known as
"a real need," — the need of change, diversion, rest,
and pleasure. And the great story-tellers, like Walter
Scott and Dumas, who do not represent a school of
thought, and do not set about a specific work of reform,
have their place quite as distinctly as George Eliot or
Charles Dickens. The story of adventure and the
romantic novel are dear to the human heart, and are
certain to reappear at intervals, no matter how marked
the occasional reaction against them may be, as long

as books are written.   Indeed, there will be a question
in many minds whether, as literary artists, some of these
occasionally discredited writers for pleasure and entertainment are not greater than those who use the novel
as a means of teaching.   That is too large a question
to discuss at this moment.   It is enough to point out
the fact that Mr. Stevenson, Mr. Crockett, Mr. Weyman,
and Mr. Doyle are in every sense legitimate novelists.
Indeed, they may point to the greatest masters of fiction as the exemplars of the particular art which they
themselves are illustrating.   Certainly the world never
needed diversion of the right sort more than it needs it
to-day, and there cannot be too many wholesome
stories of the kind that lighten the burdens, divert the
attention, and refresh the souls of men.   Art stands in
relations with life too intimate and vital to escape the
claims of contemporaneous passions, convictions, and
movements ; but the deepest notes it has struck have
issued from that fundamental human nature which lies
below the mutations of society.   " Don Quixote " is a
book for the world and for all time, not because it
satirized with such destructive power the extravagant
and over-wrought romances of chivalry, but because it
is one of those documents of human character which
are independent of the social conditions which called
them forth.

CONCERNING ORIGINALITY.

No modern man has said so many masterly things about art and the creative side of life as Goethe ; his comments and reflections form the finest body of maxims, suggestions, and principles extant, for one who seeks to know how to live fully and freely in the intellect. It is easy to point out his limitations, but it is not easy to discover the boundaries of his knowledge and activities, or to indicate the limits of his influence. He created on a great scale ; but, on a still greater scale, he rationalized and moralized the education, the materials, the methods, and the moods of the creative man among his fellows. He was not a Titan, struggling fiercely with intractable elements ; he was, rather, an Olympian, easily and calmly doing his work and living his life, with a masterful obedience to the laws of the mind, and a masterful command of his time, his talent, and his tools. In all that concerns art in its fundamental relations to the life of the artist and to society, he is the greatest modern authority.

Goethe had not only the insight, but the courage and the frankness of genius ; for genius, unlike talent, has no tricks, dexterities, or secrets of method ; it is as mysterious as the sunlight, and as open and accessible. It is true, he sometimes took a mischievous delight in mystifying his critics, but he made no secret of his methods. There was no sleight-of-hand about his skill,—it was large, free, elemental power. He used the common artistic material as freely as Shakespeare, and with as little concealment. He did not take pains to be original in the popular sense of the word. In a letter to his friend, Professor Norton, Mr. Lowell says: "The great merit, it seems to me, of the old painters was that they did not try to be original. 'To say a thing,' says Goethe, 'that everybody else has said before, as quietly as if nobody had ever said it, *that* is originality.'" The great German, who was the most profoundly original of modern men, has put this idea in several forms, and given it, by repetition, an emphasis which indicates the importance he attached to it. "There is nothing worth thinking," he says, "but it has been thought before; we must only try to think it again." In another maxim he declares that "the most foolish of all errors is for clever young men to believe that they forfeit their originality in recognizing a truth which has already been recognized by others."

The greatest minds see most clearly the long process of education which lies behind a new thought, and are quickest to know, therefore, that in the bringing of new truth to light there is always a wide division of work and a general sharing of the honor of discovery. It is, indeed, only a small mind that can produce something new in the sense that the like of it has never been seen before; for such a bit of newness can never be other than a touch of individualism, an unexpected turn of expression, a quaint phrase, an odd fancy, a fresh bit of observation. A deep thought, a wide generalization, are always based on something greater than individualism; they involve wide communion with nature or humanity. The quickly appreciated writers often have a kind of superficiality, — a telling and effective way of putting things. A fresh touch makes a familiar commonplace shine, and it passes current for the moment as a new coin; but it remains, nevertheless, the old piece whose edges have been worn these many years by much handling.

The fresh touch is something to be grateful for, but it does not evidence the possession of that rare and noble quality which we call originality. If we go to the great writers for illustration of originality, we do not find it in eccentricity of thought, in piquancy of phrase, in unusual diction, in unexpected effects of any kind. The original writers are peculiarly free from those taking mannerisms which are so constantly mistaken for evidences of originality, and so often imitated. These masters of original thought and style are singularly simple, open, and natural. Their power obviously lies in frank and unaffected expression of their own natures. For originality, like happiness, comes to those who do not seek it; to set it before one as an aim is to miss it altogether. The man who strives to be original is in grave peril of becoming sensational, and therefore, from the standpoint of art, vulgar; or, if he escapes this danger, he is likely to become self-conscious and artificial.   There is nothing more repulsive to genuine spiritual insight than the cheap and tawdry declamation which sometimes passes in the pulpit for originality, and nothing more repugnant to true artistic feeling than the posing and straining which are sometimes accepted for the moment as evidences of creative power.   Power of the highest kind is largely unconscious, and partakes too much of the nature of the divine power to be made the servant of ignoble and petty ends; and the artist whose aim is simply to catch the eye of the world will not long retain the power that is in him.

Originality of the highest and most enduring type has no tricks, mannerisms, or devices; it is elemental; it is largely unconscious; it rests, not upon individual cleverness, but upon broad and deep relationships between the artist and the world which he interprets. Homer, Dante, and Shakespeare are the most original men who have appeared in the history of literature; but they are singularly devoid of novelty in the customary sense of the word.   They are, on the contrary, singularly familiar; every reader feels that they have somehow gotten the advantage of him by expressing at an earlier age the thoughts and feelings which he had supposed to be peculiarly his own.   Nothing really great is ever unexpected; for the really great work is always based on something universal, in which every man has a share.   A conceit, a bit of quaintness, a cunning device, a sudden turn of thought or speech, takes us unaware and puzzles us; it is individual, and we have no share in it. But a great idea, or a piece of great art, finds instant recognition of its veracity and reality in the swift response of our souls. It not only speaks to us, — it speaks in us and for us. It is great because so vast a sweep of life is included in it; it is deep because it strikes below all differences of experience into the region of universal experience. Homer and Shakespeare are, in a way, as elemental as the sky which overarches all men, and which every man sees, or may see, every day of his life. But the sky is not the less wonderful because it belongs to the whole earth, and is as much the possession of the clown as of the poet. The power which hangs it before every eye has furnished no more compelling evidence of its mysterious and incalculable resources. In like manner, the highest power illustrated in art demonstrates its depth and creative force by the elemental simplicity and range of its creations, — by its insight into those things which all men possess in common. The distinctive characteristic of the man of profound originality is not that he speaks his own thought, but that he speaks my thought; not that he surprises me with novel ideas and phrases, but that he makes me acquainted with myself.

BY THE WAY.

How much of what is best and pleasantest in life comes to us by the way! The artist forms great plans and sets about great achievements, but when he comes to the hour of realization he discovers that the personal reward has come mainly by the way. The applause of which he dreamed, the fame for which he hoped, bring small satisfaction; the joy of the work was largely in the doing of it, and was taken in the long days of toil and the brief times of rest which were part of the great undertaking. To the man or woman who looks forward from the heights of youth life seems to be an artistic whole, which can be completely shaped by the will, and wrought out with perfection of detail in the repose and silence of the workshop. In that glowing time the career of a great man appears to be so symmetrical, so rounded, so complete, that it seems to be a veritable work of art, thought out and executed without hindrance, and with the co-operation of all the great forces. Nights of rest and days of work, uninterrupted and cumulative, with bursts of applause widening and deepening as the years go by, with fame adding note after note to her hymn of praise, — is not this the dream of young ambition as it surveys the field from the place of preparation?

The ideal is not an ignoble one, but it falls far short of the great reality in range and effort. There is an artistic harmony in a great life; but it is not a conscious beauty deliberately evoked by a free hand bent only on the illustration of its skill; it is a beauty born of pain, self-sacrifice, and arduous surrender to the stern conditions of success. A bit of fancy lightly inspires the singer, and as lightly borrows the wings of verse; a great vision of the imagination demands years and agonies. A bit of verse, such as serves for the small currency of poetry, runs off the pen on a convenient scrap of paper; a great poem involves a deep movement of human life, — something vast, profound, mysterious. A great life is a work of art of that noble order in which a man surrenders himself to the creative impulse, and becomes the instrument of a mightier thought and passion than he consciously originates. There is a deep sense in which we make our careers, but there is a deeper sense in which our careers are made for us. The greater the man the greater the influences that play upon him and centre in him; it is more a question of what he shall receive than of what he shall do. His life-work is wrought out in no well-appointed *atelier*, barred against intrusion, enfolded in silence; the task must be accomplished in the great arena of the world, jostled by crowds, beaten upon by storms, broken in upon by all manner of interruptions. The artist does not stand apart from his work, surveying its progress from hour to hour, and with a skilful hand bringing his thought in ever clearer view ; for the work is done, not by, but within him ; his aspiring soul, passionate heart, and eager mind are the substance upon which the tools of the graver work.   Death and care, disease and poverty, do not wait afar off, awed by greatness and enthralled by genius ; the door is always open to them, and they are often familiar companions.   The work of a great life is always accomplished with toil, self-sacrifice, and with incessant intrusions from without ; it is often accomplished amid bitter sorrows and under the pressure of relentless misfortune.

Yet these things, that break in upon the artistic mood and play havoc with the artistic poise, make the life-work immeasurably nobler and richer ; the reality differs from the ideal of youth in being vaster, and therefore more difficult and painful of attainment. The easy achievement, always well in hand, and executed in the quiet of reposeful hours, gives place to the sublime accomplishment wrought out amid the uproar of the world and under the pressure of the sorrow and anguish which are a part of every human lot.   The toil is intense, prolonged, and painful because it is to be imperishable ; there is a divine element in it, and the work takes on a form of immortality.   The little time which falls to the artist here is inadequate to the greatness of his task ; the applause, small or great, which accompanies his toil is but a momentary and imperfect recognition of what has been done with strength and beauty. It is pleasant when men see what one has done, but the real satisfaction is the consciousness that something worthy of being seen has been accomplished. The rewards of great living are not external things, withheld until the crowning hour of success arrives; they come by the way, — in the consciousness of growing power and worth, of duties nobly met, and work thoroughly done. To the true artist, working always in humility and sincerity, all life is a reward, and every day brings a deeper satisfaction. Joy and peace are by the way.

THE END.